THE HUNT

THE HUNT

KIMBERLY A. BETTES

CP
CASE PUBLISHING
USA

Copyright © 2019 Kimberly A. Bettes
Cover design © 2019 Kimberly A. Bettes

Published by Case Publishing, USA.

For Anita, the warrior

and

For Luke who loves Susan,
Susan who loves Luke,
And Hope who tolerates them both.

FOREWORD

I recently held a benefit for my mother in-law, Anita. She's battling lung cancer for the second time. It's her third time fighting cancer, and each time has drained her physically and financially.

Hence, the benefit.

One of the things I did for the benefit was sell the opportunity to be a main character in a book. I planned to auction it during the live auction portion of the benefit, but then I remembered that I had a huge fan in Luke Davis. I went to his wife Susan, and we struck a deal behind his back. She donated money to the cause, and I wrote a book for Luke. Huge surprise to him, I'm sure. (Hi, Luke. Hope you enjoy the story.)

I tell you that to tell you this.

Anita is still fighting. We almost lost her shortly after the benefit, but she's not one to go quietly into that good night. However, the war is taking its toll. If you would like to donate money to her for the expenses she's incurring (doctor bills, trips to chemo, etc.), please send them to me via Paypal (kimberlyabettes@yahoo.com) or Facebook, and I will see that she gets them. For other forms of payment, you can email me or contact me through any of my social media accounts. Every little bit helps, as I'm sure you know. Thank you so much.

Kim

PS I will repeat this message at the end of the book to remind you that Anita needs all the support she can get. Enjoy the story, and thank you in advance for your help.

chapter **ONE**

The mid-November sun hung low in the sky, offering up its last few moments of warmth from behind the bare treetops. Luke Davis stood on his porch, hands buried deep in the pockets of his coat. He bounced up on his toes a few times, trying to keep his blood pumping and his body warm. Inhaling deeply through his nose, he held his breath for a moment, felt the icy sting of the cold air deep in his lungs, and then exhaled, watching the cloud of expelled air fade away into the brisk breeze.

This is insane, he thought.

He glanced down the driveway, saw nothing between his house and the street, and shook his head. "Screw this," he mumbled, turning to head back inside.

He must've been crazy to think waiting on the porch was a good idea. Luke knew how Tom was. The two had been friends since they were ten years old, almost four whole decades now, and neither of them had changed much in all that time. Luke knew that Tom's be-there-in-a-minute might turn out to be three hours. Maybe more. So far, half an hour had passed since the two spoke on the phone, Tom Wilkins promising to pick up Luke *in a minute*. Half an hour in which there had been no sign whatsoever of Tom.

Luke headed inside, his fingers wrapping around the cold door knob, ready to turn it and smell the delicious aroma of Susan's meatloaf hanging heavy in the warm air of the home they'd made together. Before he could open the door, however, he heard an engine getting louder as it grew closer. Turning, he saw Tom's black Ford F-150 coming up the driveway. He watched as it pulled to a stop, both the driver and the passenger laughing from behind the windshield.

Tom rolled down the window as Luke walked toward the truck. "Get in, whistlepig." He laughed, pulled his head back inside the cab, and rolled up the window.

Though he was aggravated at his friend's tardiness, Luke flashed a half-hearted grin and walked around the front of the truck to the passenger side, thinking about how long it had been since anyone had called him whistlepig. His name was James Lucas, but everyone called him Luke. Whistlepig was a nickname that had been adopted mostly by the older folks around town back in the day. The only person who still called him that was Tom's dad. And, of course, Tom.

Luke pulled open the door, picked up the empty soda bottle that rolled out and fell onto the ground, and tossed it into the bed of the truck, where it landed along many other empty cans and bottles. Luke waited until Roy Johnston slid across the seat and settled in next to Tom before he climbed into the cab and shut the door.

"It stinks in here," Luke said, after breathing in through his nose and immediately wishing he hadn't.

Putting the truck in reverse and backing out of the driveway, Tom said, "That there's deer piss and excitement you're smellin'."

"Really? It smells more like bullshit and desperation to me," Luke said jokingly. What it really smelled like was body odor, booze, and cigarette smoke. The body odor could've come from either or both of the men, but the booze and cigarettes were all Roy's doing.

"I'll take your word for it, Bloodhound," Tom said with a smile as he pulled onto the street and drove away from Luke's house.

Bloodhound. Another moniker Luke had acquired over the years, earned for his innate ability to track things down. Particularly animals his friends had shot. Contrary to what most folks believed, animals didn't just drop where they stood when a bullet or an arrow entered their body. They jerked and bucked and ran off into the woods, adrenaline mixing with their fear and giving them one last boost of energy to get as far away from the noise and the pain as they could. Sometimes, they didn't make it very far before collapsing onto the ground and dying. Other times, they made it a seemingly impossible distance away, which is when Luke's phone would ring, and he'd have to go track down the animal's carcass so it could be harvested properly. It had happened so often over the years, he'd become known around town as Bloodhound Luke.

Shoulder to shoulder, the men sat, scrunched together on the worn bench seat of the pickup truck. Tom was by far the largest of the three. He was little more than five and a half feet tall, but what he lacked in height he made up for in weight. If the scale showed less than four hundred pounds when he stepped on it, that scale was broken.

Roy, on the other hand, was a few inches over six feet tall and most likely didn't get anywhere near a hundred and seventy-five pounds, even if he stepped on the scale wearing everything he owned. The man seemed to consist of nothing but thin bones and even thinner skin.

Luke fell somewhere in between the other two. He was neither tall nor short, fat nor skinny. He was just under six feet tall and weighed just under two hundred pounds. Mostly muscle, to hear Luke tell it.

"I hope you told Susan you weren't coming home tonight," Tom said, lifting his index finger off the steering wheel to give a Missouri hello to a passing vehicle.

"Bull shit," Luke said. "It's meatloaf night. I'm not missing that for anything."

Roy said, "I'm afraid you might miss it tonight."

Luke studied Roy's face, trying to determine whether or not his friend was joking. Unable to decide, he finally asked, "Are you serious?"

Roy nodded his head as Tom replied, "You betcha. I'll be surprised if we find the damn thing before midnight. It'd take a

3

whole lotta luck. And I may be a lot of things, boy, but lucky ain't one of 'em."

"I'll be surprised if we find it at all," Roy said.

"No shit?" Luke asked, almost able to taste the meatloaf he was going to miss. Wishing he hadn't answered the phone when Tom called, he asked, "So what exactly happened?"

It was as if he'd been waiting for someone to ask. The words had barely left Luke's mouth when Tom said, "Twelve-point buck walked right in front of my scope. I threw up my gun, put my cross-hairs on it, and pulled the trigger, you know. I figured it would drop right there because it was a hell of a shot. I mean I hit that sucker dead on. Oh, it was beautiful. But the damn thing took off like a scalded ass rabbit. I figured hell, that wasn't no big deal. They do that sort of thing all the time. So I listened to see how far it ran, and I'll tell you what, boy. That damned thing never did stop." Tom slapped the steering wheel for emphasis.

"It never stopped, huh?" Luke asked.

"Never did," Tom replied. "It just kept crashing through the woods, crunching leaves and snapping twigs like a group of mental patients on a hike. But I know I shot it. I saw it happen. Saw the damn thing buck like an angry bronco. Me and Roy followed the blood trail till we lost it. I told him hell, let's just go back to the truck and come to town and get ol' bloodhound Luke. If anybody can find it, I know he can. Everybody knows how good you are at following them blood trails."

Roy looked at Luke and smiled broadly, revealing uneven teeth, yellowed from decades of smoking and poor dental hygiene. He said, "Ol' bloodhound Luke." Then he laughed. It wasn't loud, but it was more of a cackle. Luke had always hated Roy's laugh. Now was no different.

Luke turned his attention from Tom and Roy to the road ahead, looking past the crack in the windshield that ran directly through his line of sight and focusing on the street beyond.

They stopped at a convenience store on the edge of town for gas and to load up on snacks and drinks before heading out to the woods to track down the deer. Tom stood at the pump, filling the truck while Roy and Luke went inside the store. Once inside, they went their separate ways, roaming up and down the aisles until they found everything they were looking for.

4

While Luke and Roy sought out their snacks of choice, the employees at the front of the store talked about a story that had been in the headlines for a week or so. Luke absentmindedly listened in, scanning the shelves for whatever goodies looked appealing to him.

"I heard they found him," one female employee said.

"No," responded a different woman. "I watched the news at noon today, and they said they were still looking for him."

"Do they know who they're looking for? Like, is it a family member or someone that knew him?"

"I don't think they know who it was that took him. There was one witness who said they saw him get into a red truck, but then there was another who said it was a white van. So who knows?"

"Why is it always a white van? Every time a kid goes missing, it's always a white van. Have you noticed that?"

"I know, right? I was terrified of white vans until I was, like, twenty-five."

"I'm thirty-two, and I'm still scared of them," said the other woman.

They laughed.

"I hope they find him. What is he, six?"

"I think they said he's seven."

"Geez. That's terrible. And you know the longer they search, the less the chances of them finding him alive."

"I know. I hate it for his family. Can you imagine?"

A man interrupted their conversation to say he'd got gas on pump six. As the cashier hit buttons and the register beeped, the man asked, "You guys talkin' about that boy that's missin' from Poplar Bluff?"

"Yeah," the women answered in unison.

"Isn't it sad?" asked the younger of the employees.

"They won't find him," the man said.

The man's answer made Luke forget about snacks for the moment. He looked toward the front of the store, staring over the top of the shelves at the back of the man's head. Luke didn't recognize him. At least not without seeing the guy's face. He was tall and thin with closely-cropped dark hair. He could've been anybody, but he didn't seem to be anyone Luke knew.

Luke thought the man's statement was an odd thing to say, especially when talking about a missing kid. And judging by the look on the women's faces, they were thinking the same thing.

One of them asked, "What do you mean?"

The man replied with a shrug, "He's been missin' for over a week. If they were goin' to find him, they would've found him by now. I'd say he's hidden away pretty damn good, wouldn't you?"

The women looked at each other, not knowing how to respond to such a peculiar response.

The man, seeing their expressions, put their minds at ease when he added, "I watch a lot of television. True crime and all that."

His explanation seemed to sit well with the women. Luke watched as they relaxed, breathing a visible sigh of relief and smiling at the man as he paid cash for his gas and left.

Luke was taken away from the scene at the front of the store when Roy came up beside him and said, "Look here. Look at the size of this pepperoni stick." He held it out so Luke could feast his eyes upon it.

"Yeah. That's pretty big."

With a laugh, Roy said, "That's what all the ladies tell me." He slapped Luke on the shoulder and cackled. Then he said, "I'm gonna get a bunch of these. You want any?"

"No," Luke said. "I'm not in the mood for pepperoni." What he was in the mood for was meatloaf, but that was back at his house. He'd have to settle for something else, something less filling and far less delicious.

Roy bought a fistful of the over-sized pepperoni sticks, a bag of beef jerky, a king size candy bar, and a cup of soda from the fountain on the far wall.

Luke decided that if he was going to be out for a long time, possibly all night, he would need more than just a candy bar, so he grabbed one of the pre-cooked hamburgers from the heated display case, two bags of salted peanuts, a bottle of soda from the cooler at the back of the store, and a little something for his daughter Hope. He then got in line behind Roy and waited patiently for his turn to pay, watching through the glass doors as Tom returned the nozzle to the pump and made his way across the parking lot, coughing along the way.

6

Roy paid for his things, gathered up his items, and moved to the side, stuffing his snacks into various pockets of his clothing as Luke stepped forward and plopped his goodies onto the counter. After he paid, Luke gathered his items, tucking Hope's snack into his breast pocket, where it would be close to his heart. It wasn't something he thought about doing, just a subconscious move that showed how he felt about the girl.

Luke and Roy returned to the truck and waited for Tom. It took him a long time to return, and when he did, he was carrying a bottle of soda in one hand and a white plastic bag filled to capacity in the other. He was walking quicker now than when he had entered the store minutes earlier, and he was smiling broadly.

"Glad we got our snacks first," Luke said, watching out the window as the bag swung heavily in Tom's hand. "I don't think he left anything in there for anybody else."

"Doesn't look like it," Roy said. "What do you suppose he's smilin' about?"

"I'm not sure. Maybe there was a sale on snack cakes."

Roy cackled, making Luke wish he hadn't said something funny.

Tom rounded the front of the truck and jerked open the driver's door. "Change of plans, fellers," he said as he tossed his bag inside. He scrunched himself in behind the steering wheel and shut the door without saying another word.

"Change of plans?" Luke asked, leaning forward to see around Roy. He hoped Tom would say he'd decided to forget about the deer and call it a night. But the look on his face and the excitement in his tone suggested that he had other things on his mind.

"You see them guys over there?" Tom pointed to the opposite side of the parking lot where two men stood next to a pick-up, talking.

Roy and Luke turned and looked, studying the guys Tom was referring to.

"What about 'em," asked Roy.

Tom said, "I overheard them talkin' inside, so I stuck around to listen. You know what they're getting ready to do? They're goin' huntin'."

"Hunting?" Luke asked, confused. "It's too late to go hunting."

7

Roy chimed in, "I believe they call it spotlighting."

"If they get caught," Luke said, "they'll get a big fine. Lose their license. And their guns. That's not a good idea..." He wasn't sure why his friend was so excited to see a group of guys breaking the law, but he waited to find out more.

Nodding, Tom said, "It is too late to go deer huntin'. But they're not goin' deer huntin'."

After thinking about it, Luke said, "It's too late to do any hunting. Hunting in the dark is illegal. Not to mention it's a bad idea."

"It's called spotlighting," Roy said with a smile.

"Damn it, Roy," Luke said. "I know what it's called."

"But this ain't any type of huntin' the state of Missouri has any say in," Tom said, his smile widening.

Finally, Luke caved and asked, "Tom, what the hell are you talking about?"

He lowered his voice, not wanting anyone but Luke and Roy to hear, even though there was no one else around. "They're huntin' a monster," he said, as if those four words told Luke everything he needed to know.

"A monster?" Roy asked.

Tom nodded. "That's right. A monster."

Luke's mind raced. He hadn't believed in monsters since he was five years old. He looked at Tom, wondering if perhaps his friend was having a stroke of some sort or perhaps had taken drugs. The kind that made you see man-eating plants and purple dragons and monsters in the corner.

Tom, seeing the confusion on their faces, continued. "You guys hear about what's been going on over by Lesterville?" Without waiting for them to respond, he continued, "Someone's been vandal-izin' property all over the place. Mostly folks' houses and campers and stuff like that. Not a lot of damage to the city, except overturned trash cans and dumpsters. But it ain't the property that's got people up in arms. It's the animals."

"Animals?" Roy asked.

"It started out killin' cats and dogs. Ripped 'em to shreds. Nothin' left but a pile of bloody fur. Then it moved on to bigger things, like goats and pigs and cows. Tore through my buddy Jim's herd last week. He had fifty head of black angus Thursday night when he went to bed. Woke up with forty-two. Wasn't much left of the other eight."

"What's been doin' it?" Roy asked.

"Nobody knows," said Tom. "Some people think it's a big-foot."

"Oh, Jesus," Luke said, blowing a puff of air through his lips and rolling his eyes.

"What?" Tom asked, offended by Luke's reaction. "All that stuff has really happened."

"I'm sure it has," Luke replied. "But I seriously doubt it's the work of a sasquatch."

"Well what do you think did it?"

"I don't know. A group of teenagers, maybe. Or some doped-up crackheads. But not a bigfoot."

"Why can't it be a bigfoot?" Roy asked.

"Because it can't be something that doesn't exist," Luke scoffed.

"Well," Tom said, "it's damn sure somethin' makin' all that trouble. And the worst thing of all is, over by Bunker, it killed a little girl."

"What?" Roy asked, his voice rising an octave. "It killed a little girl? When?"

"No way," Luke said, shaking his head. "I would've heard about that."

Nodding once to confirm that he spoke the truth, Tom said, "It happened just this morning. Little girl was waiting on the school bus at the end of the driveway when the damn thing attacked her. The girl's father is pissed. He wants it. Dead or alive." When neither Luke nor Roy said anything, Tom added, "He's offering a reward."

Silence filled the cab of the truck.

Roy and Luke looked at each other, then looked back at Tom.

All Luke could think about was how the father must've felt, about how awful it must be to lose a child in such a horrific way. Losing them in any way was bad enough, but to lose one so tragical-ly...And that poor girl. Just waiting on the school bus, either excited about or dreading another day at school with her friends, and then *wham!* She was dead. Gone forever. And so viciously.

9

Beside him, Roy was focused on something other than the heartbreak of the tragedy. It was evident when he broke the silence by asking, "How much of a reward are we talkin' here?"

"Twenty-five thousand dollars. Cash." Tom's eyebrows rose high on his broad forehead as he spoke, his eyes shining bright with intensity and excitement.

"That's a lot of money," Roy said wistfully. "I could do a lot of things with that kind of dough."

"Damn right, it's a lot of money," Tom agreed. "Even split three ways, it's…" He trailed off, unable to do the math in his mind. "Well that's, uh…Let's see here…"

Luke said, "Eight thousand three hundred thirty-three dollars apiece. And thirty-three cents." His thoughts turned from the horrors of having a child mauled to death by an animal to what he could do for his own daughter with that kind of money. Savings. College. A car for her sixteenth birthday, which was coming up much sooner than Luke cared to admit. He didn't like the way it made him feel, thinking of money and how it could benefit him, all at the expense of a family who had lost so much, but he couldn't stop his mind from racing.

"How do they know what they're looking for?" Luke asked, unwilling to risk killing an innocent creature for a little bit of money. No matter how much he could use it.

Tom replied, "The girl's father heard her screams, grabbed a rifle, and ran out of the house. He saw it standin' over his little girl, eating her. He ran toward it, firing off a couple shots as he went. The first shot didn't scare it. After the second shot, it took off. He didn't get a good look at it, but he saw enough to know that it was covered in dark hair, made godawful sounds, and it was big. Bigger than anything around here could possibly be."

"Just like the one in Lesterville," muttered Roy. When he realized his words had captured the attention of Tom and Luke, he added, "They were talkin' about it in the bar the other night. I figured it was a bunch of bullshit. Just some bar talk, you know? But they were sayin' that some people had seen it run across the road over by Black River Bridge. They said the same thing, that it was covered in dark fur and was huge."

"Were there witnesses to any of the vandalism in Lesterville?" Luke asked.

"I don't think so," Tom replied. "I heard someone got a picture of something on their trail camera, but it was too blurry to make out what it was. All they could tell was that it was big and dark."

"Gotta be a bigfoot," Roy said.

"Oh, come on," Luke said, shaking his head.

"What?" Roy asked. "Bigfoot is real."

"I suppose you believe in Santa Claus, the Easter Bunny, the Tooth Fairy, and leprechauns too, huh, Roy?" Luke asked.

"I don't believe in Sannie Claus or the egg rabbit or the tooth collector, but them leppercorns are real."

"Leprechauns," Luke corrected.

"That's what I said. Leppercorns."

Rolling his eyes, Luke said, "All this technology around us, yet no one can ever get a picture or a video of a bigfoot. That's pretty convenient, don't you think?"

Roy shrugged. "Maybe the bigfoots are smart enough to avoid cameras."

"Right. Because a half-man half-animal hybrid who lives deep in the woods and has no sense of civilization not only knows what a camera is but also knows it should avoid them to prevent exposing itself to society. Makes about as much sense as dumping ice in a volcano to stop the lava flow."

Before Roy could respond to Luke, Tom said, "Well apparently this damn thing ain't afraid of nothin'. Barkin' dogs sure the hell don't scare it. A herd of angry angus didn't ruffle its feathers none."

"I thought you said it had hair, not feathers," Luke said sarcastically.

Paying no attention to Luke's interjection, Tom continued, "And from the sounds of it, neither do gunshots."

"But why would a bigfoot eat a human?" Roy asked. "They don't do that. They eat, I don't know, berries and…other berries." He struggled to recall all his knowledge of bigfoots—or was it bigfeet?—and what they ate, but he couldn't think of anything other than berries. But he knew for sure that people weren't on the list.

"Who the hell knows why? Animals go crazy and do shit like this all the time," Tom said.

Roy thought for a minute, and then he said, "What if ain't a bigfoot? What if it's one of them chabbacupras?"

11

Tom said, "You mean choppercobra."

Sighing, Luke said, "My god, you two are illiterate. It's Chupacabra."

"That's what I said," Roy replied. "Chabbacupra. What if it's one of them doin' it?"

"It's not a Chupacabra," Luke said.

"How do you know?" Roy asked.

"Because those aren't real either," Luke said.

Roy looked at him, frowning. "How sad it must be to not believe in anything."

"I believe in stuff. Stuff that exists."

The men looked at each other, thinking about all that had been said.

Then, ignoring their discussion on what was real and what wasn't, Tom asked, "So what do you fellas say? You wanna go catch this thing before it kills someone else's little girl?" Looking directly at Luke, he added, "Whether or not it's a bigfoot or a choppercobra, it will kill again. Unless we stop it."

"Hell yeah," Roy said, slapping his hands together. "Let's go get this son of a bitch. I could really use the money."

Luke was more reluctant in his response. If the thing had just been damaging property, he would've said no. But it had killed pets, and now it had started killing children. He couldn't let that stand. He couldn't go home and look his daughter in the eyes without knowing he had done everything in his power to protect her and all the other children in the county from suffering the same fate as the little girl in Bunker. And Tom was right. It didn't matter what it was. It had to be stopped, one way or another.

Nodding slowly, Luke looked at Roy and then at Tom. "Yeah," he said. "Let's go get it."

They left the convenience store parking lot and headed out of town as dusk settled on the Ozark Mountains, casting shadows on the land that grew larger and darker until they all merged into one black mass known as night.

chapter **TWO**

Tom followed the faded ribbon of blacktop that twisted around curves, over hills, and through valleys until the pavement disappeared and the road turned to dirt. He then reduced his speed a bit and drove on, gravel pinging against the undercarriage of the truck as the men inside the cab joked and laughed about work and women and the good old days when they were young and in the prime of their lives. Anything to take their minds off the image of a little girl being ripped to shreds by a wild animal.

Luke missed the days when they were young. When his bones didn't creak and sleeping wrong wasn't a thing that could happen. Back when they were all fit and strong. Even Tom, who had always been chunkier than Luke and Roy but nowhere near as large as he was now.

The three men had shared the majority of their lives and memories with each other. They had been nearly inseparable until their teen years, when girls entered the picture. Then, less and less time was spent with each other and more of it was spent with people of the opposite sex. It hadn't taken Luke long to find the right girl in Susan, but it had taken Tom and Roy quite a while to find their Miss

Right. Both men often claimed they were playing the field and sowing their wild oats, but what they had really been doing was trying to find a girl who would put up with them for more than a couple of dates. Eventually, Roy and Tom each found their own special girl, and all three men, once joined at the hip, got married and made new lives that didn't include seeing much of each other.

"Hey," Tom said to Luke, an idea obviously just occurring to him. "You'll never guess who I ran into the other day."

After tucking a wad of chewing tobacco between his cheek and gum, Luke asked, "Who's that?"

"Julio."

Luke's eyebrows went up. "Oh yeah? Damn. I haven't seen him in...shit. I guess it's been a few years now." Images of Carl, nicknamed Julio, flooded Luke's mind. Things they'd done. Jokes they'd shared.

"I see him about once a year or so," Tom said before taking a drink of his soda and returning it to its place between his thick legs. He belched and said, "He looks the same now as he did in high school. I don't know what his secret is, but he ain't aged a day." He leaned forward, looking past Roy to Luke, and said, "Unlike you. Your hair looks like you fell in a sack full of damp flour."

Tom laughed loudly at his own joke, obviously pleased with himself for making fun of Luke's hair, which was nowhere near as white as the large man would have you believe. Sure, Luke was beginning to gray at the temples, but it wasn't much. The crow's feet hadn't found his eyes yet, and his skin didn't look like worn leather, so he felt he was doing pretty good in the aging department. He may not get carded when buying alcohol anymore, but he knew damn well he could pass for ten years younger than he was. Unlike Tom, who hadn't been asked to verify he was old enough to buy booze since he was a teenager. Luke had often pondered the notion that Tom Wilkins had, in fact, been born old. He thought about saying something to that effect now but decided that instead of making jabs about his friend's appearance, he'd ask about the man with whom they had shared so many good times over the years.

"Ol' Julio. How's he doing, anyway?" Luke unscrewed the cap from his empty soda bottle and spat tobacco juice into it.

"He's doing fine. Kids are grown and in college. He's divorced and remarried. They live over in Doniphan now. She's got

14

kids that are in college too. I'd hate to have those bills," Tom said before laughing.

"No shit," Roy agreed. "Glad I don't have that problem."

There were a lot of problems that Roy didn't have because he'd never had kids. Looking at him now, Luke thought that even if he and his wife had spawned a dozen little Johnstons, they still wouldn't have been saddled with such bills because none of them would've made it out of high school, much less into college. He didn't say that though. He liked Roy and didn't want to insult him or start a fight. Especially not now.

Luke sat silent for a moment, his mind flooding with memories. "Boy, we had some fun, didn't we?"

Roy answered, "We sure did."

Tom, suddenly struck by another thought, said, "Hey, Whistlepig, remember that time you ran down Main Street naked? What the hell was that all about?"

"Weren't you there?" Roy asked Tom.

"Nope. But I sure as hell heard about it the next day. And a whole bunch of days after that." He laughed loudly, his voice booming inside the cab of the truck. He leaned forward and pounded the steering wheel to emphasize his hilarity.

"I sure thought you were there," Roy said, trailing off. "Oh, no. I'm thinking of Peterhead. He was there."

"Hell, Peterhead was always there," Tom said, laughing himself into a coughing fit.

Luke said, "Everybody was there. Except you, apparently." He spat into the bottle again. Every time he chewed tobacco, he heard Susan telling him he should stop. She didn't nag him about it because that's not the kind of woman she was, but she had made it known throughout the years that the habit disgusted her. Every time he chewed tobacco, every time he spat, he thought of quitting. For her.

"Speakin' of Peterhead," Tom said, "I called him before I called you to see if he would come out here with us."

"I take it he told you to go to hell," Luke replied. "Which, by the way, is what I should've done."

"Nah. He wasn't home. Him and his boy hadn't got home from huntin' yet," Tom said before taking another drink of soda and belching again.

"You're one sexy son of a bitch, Tom," Roy said, cackling.

"That's what your wife tells me," Tom quipped, turning to give Roy a wink before laughing noisily again. His laugh was booming, the kind that would fill a room, no matter the size. It was especially harsh on the ears in the small cab of the truck.

Though Luke liked hanging out with his friends, he sure wished Dwain, known to the gang as Peterhead, would have agreed to come out with Tom and Roy. Then Luke could've stayed home and gorged himself on meatloaf instead of snacking on a dry hamburger and salted peanuts that tasted like they were a couple months past their prime. He sighed, staring through the cracked windshield as they headed deeper into the wilds of the cold, dark Ozarks and farther away from the cozy comforts of home.

After a few minutes of silence, Luke asked, "So do you think we'll find it?"

Tom must've been thinking the same thing because he instantly shrugged and said, "It seems to be makin' an appearance all over the county. And it's not afraid of anything, so it shouldn't be hard to find."

Roy asked, "Where do we even start? I mean, it could be anywhere by now."

"I figure we'll go to where it got the girl this morning. Maybe we can find some tracks or something. Figure out which way it headed and go from there. That sound good to you, Bloodhound?" Tom asked, leaning forward to see around Roy.

"Sounds about as good anything I can come up with," Luke agreed.

When Tom stopped the truck and killed the lights and the engine, Luke stepped out and moved aside so Roy could follow him. He stretched, spat his wad of tobacco onto the ground, and waited for Tom to get out and make his way around the truck to join them.

Watching Roy climb down out of the truck, Luke laughed.

"What's so funny?" Roy asked.

"You. What the hell are you wearing?"

Roy looked down at his attire. A bright orange safety vest over top of camouflage coveralls, camo boots, and a camo fanny pack. Looking back at Luke, he asked, "What's wrong with it?"

"You're wearing a fanny pack. Like a little girl. In the nineteen eighties."

"Yeah, but check this out." Roy unzipped the fanny pack and reached inside. He pulled a can of beer out and held it up for Luke to see.

"Okay, but you—"

"Wait," Roy interjected. With his other hand, he reached into the fanny pack and pulled out another can of beer.

"Only you, Roy," Luke said with a sigh. "I think what makes it look so...I don't know, stupid, is that you're wearing the fanny pack on top of your coveralls. It looked goofy as hell."

"You know what I think?" Roy asked, returning the cans of alcohol to the waist purse. "I think you're just jealous because you ain't cool enough to pull off wearin' one of these bad boys."

Nodding, Luke said, "Yeah, Roy. That's probably it."

As Tom came around the truck, Roy turned his back to Luke and relieved himself. While he was doing that, Luke pulled his cell phone out of his pocket and began to place a call to Susan.

"You might as well put that thing away," Tom said.

"Why's that? The size of it make you jealous?" Roy asked with a cackle.

"I was talkin' to Whistlepig," Tom said. "Roy, you can keep playin' with yours." To Luke, he added, "There ain't no service out here."

To verify the man's statement, Luke checked his screen and saw that Tom was right. There was no service. The only cell tower in the area was many miles away, at the top of a steep hill on the far side of the county. They were in a valley entirely too far away for the device to be of any use to him. So much for letting his wife know he was going to be a while, and so much for asking her to save him some meatloaf. He returned the phone to his pocket and sighed. Why hadn't he called her from the gas station? Better yet, why the hell had he answered the phone when Tom called?

"Well how'd you call me?" Luke asked. "You shot that deer in the woods. How'd you manage to find a signal to call me?"

"I called you from town," Tom said, handing Luke a head-lamp.

"You called me from town, yet it still took you over half an hour to get to my house? I live in town, Tom. What the hell took you so long? Town is not that big." Less than a thousand people lived inside the city limits. There were only a handful of streets and busi-

17

nesses. You could casually walk across the entire town in fifteen minutes.

"Hell, I don't know," Tom said with a shrug. "This and that, I reckon."

Roy turned back to the men and said, "It's my fault. He had to come in and explain to Linda why we were late getting' home."

Luke nodded. That story checked out with him because he knew how Roy's wife Linda was. And he also knew she had a good reason to be that way.

"Yeah, it seems she doesn't believe ol' Roy here when he tells her somethin'." Looking at Roy, Tom asked, "Now why do you suppose that is, Roy? Huh? Why don't she believe anything you say?"

Roy looked down at his feet.

"Is it because you're a lyin' sack of horse shit?" Tom asked, wrapping his thick arm around his friend's thin shoulders.

Raising his head abruptly, Roy snapped, "One time! I only lied one time."

"Now, Roy," Tom said.

"It's true. It was just the once."

"But that was a damn big lie, wasn't it? And it encompassed about a million little lies, didn't it?"

Roy hung his head again.

Tom slapped Roy's back and laughed. "Oh, hell, son. I'm just bustin' your balls. Me and ol' Whistlepig here know how women are, don't we, Luke?"

"Don't include me in your filthy web of lies. I don't have woman troubles like the two of you clowns do," Luke said, pulling the headlamp onto his head and adjusting it for a secure fit.

Luke and Susan got along great. They always had. Meanwhile, Tom and his wife got along much better in the years since their divorce than they ever had while they were married. And though Roy and his wife had never got along together, things had been especially rocky between the two since he got busted cheating on her. Now, she never believed anything he told her. And really, who could blame her?

"Where are we, anyway?" Luke asked.

"You know where Hanks Holler is?" Tom replied.

18

"Hanks Hollow? Oh shit," Luke said. "That's way the hell out there."

Tom said, "Yeah, well, we're way the hell past that."

"What?" Luke asked, his voice coming out at a much higher pitch than he would've liked. "Past Hanks Hollow? You're kidding."

"Calm down, Luke. Damn. You're like one of those old explorers who thought the other side of over there was the end of the world. Trust me, son. You ain't gonna fall off," Tom said, laughing.

"And there ain't no dragons here," Roy added. "At least none that we know of."

"Why am I not surprised that you believe in dragons too, Roy?" Luke asked, pulling gloves out of his pocket and sliding them on his hands.

With a shrug and a grin, Roy said, "What can I say? I'm a believer."

It's not that Luke was afraid of falling off the edge of the world. And he didn't expect to find any dragons, either. He wasn't an idiot. It was just that he didn't want to be there. At all. He didn't want to be out in the cold. In the dark. In the woods. Hunting a dangerous animal with a guy who was already three sheets to the wind and another guy who got winded putting on his socks. He wanted to be at home with Susan and Hope and a big plate of meatloaf, damn it.

The temperature had already dropped a few degrees, and it wouldn't take long for it to drop even further. Though he'd dressed for the weather, the chill of the night air still bit at his face, the only part of his body that was left exposed. Everything else was covered in warm layers.

The other men were dressed for warmth as well. They had been hunting earlier in the day and hadn't bothered to change clothes. Looking at them now, an idea occurred to Luke.

"Should I be wearing bright orange too, you think?" he asked.

"Nah," Tom said with a wave of his hand. "You can't see it in the dark anyway. Plus, nobody's supposed to be huntin' now. It's after sundown. That's illegal. Remember?" He grinned at Luke.

Luke shrugged. "Alright then. When the coroner comes to collect my bloody body, you assholes make sure to tell him that I don't need an autopsy because I died of a gunshot wound, even though Tom here said it was after sundown and I didn't need any orange because you couldn't see it anyway."

Tom and Roy laughed, Tom doubling over and holding his oversized belly, wheezing and gasping for air, Roy with his head thrown back, cackling at the sky.

In the minute or so it took the two men to settle down, Luke turned on the headlamp and adjusted the beam of light so it was shining on the ground in front of his feet. When their laughter faded, he said, "You know, the fact isn't lost on me that not only am I the only one of us not wearing safety orange, I'm also the only one who doesn't have a gun."

"Oh, hell. We'll be fine," Tom said, still wheezing.

Luke replied, "I know *you'll* be fine. *You* have a gun. I don't. You're both armed while I'm standing here with nothing more than a flashlight and a prayer."

"Don't worry about it, buddy," Roy said, reaching into the bed of the truck where he fished a cold can of beer from a cooler. He popped the top, took a long drink, and belched before smiling at Luke and saying, "We have your back."

Dryly, Luke said, "That doesn't make me feel any better." A drunk guy having his back didn't exactly give Luke a sense of security.

Roy hadn't always been an alcoholic. Just since he was a teenager. Giving credit where credit was due, Luke had to admit that Roy was a high-functioning alcoholic. Had he not reeked of beer, you probably wouldn't even know he was drunk. But he always reeked of the stuff because he was always drunk.

"This is it, boys," Tom said, strapping his headlamp onto his head. He fumbled for the button, found it, and switched the thing on. The beam shone directly in Luke's eyes.

"Damn it, Tom," Luke said, turning his head and squeezing his eyes shut. When he opened them, little white circles hovered in the center of his vision for several seconds before gradually fading away.

"Sorry about that. I'm still gettin' used to this stupid thing. But hey, it frees up my hands for other things. Like shootin' rabid bigfoots and choppercobras."

The thought that the...whatever it was they were looking for might be rabid hadn't crossed Luke's mind until now. He wasn't sure if all animals could get rabies, but he didn't see why they couldn't. Humans could get it, as well as racoons and dogs and cats, so why not everything else?

Roy stepped over to the mailbox that stood at the edge of the road. It was a black metal box with gold letters stuck to the side of it that spelled out the name Ramshaw. "This is where it happened, huh?"

"Yeah. This is it," Tom said. He walked around Roy, adjusting his headlamp until it illuminated the ground in front of him. When Tom stopped walking, the beam of light atop his head fell directly on the spot where someone's baby girl had been slaughtered that very morning.

Luke's heart sank, and his throat tightened at the sight.

It was real now. It was no longer a story they'd heard or a rumor going around town. It was a real thing that really happened to real people. People whose hearts were now broken. People who sat in a house at the end of this very driveway, crying their eyes out and wishing like hell their little girl was back with them.

They had all expected there would be blood, but none of them expected there would be so much of it. Even though the attack had happened that morning, about twelve hours earlier, the blood was still there and still that easily recognizable shade of deep crimson. It hadn't dried, hadn't turned the brownish black color that blood turns after prolonged exposure to air, and it hadn't been absorbed by the ground. In the cold November temperature, the pool of blood had simply frozen atop the earth. A horrible moment standing still in time, like a grotesque snapshot.

Unable to stomach the sight of so much gore, Luke averted his eyes, focusing instead on the area around the blood. That was when he saw the other things. The hair barrette. The box of spilled crayons, some of which were broken. The pink lunchbox with its contents strewn across the driveway and trampled. He found those things even harder to look at than the blood. The sadness harder to stomach than the gore.

"We have got to kill that fuckin' thing," Tom said solemnly, all traces of his jovial personality now gone.

"Yes we do," Roy agreed.

"And we will," Luke said with certainty.

21

chapter **THREE**

       After leaving the Ramshaw place where the little girl had met her grisly end, the men drove in the direction where Tom thought the animal must've gone. They hadn't found any tracks leading away from the scene of the attack, but Luke didn't figure it mattered much. The thing could be anywhere by now, and they had to start looking somewhere, so wherever Tom stopped the truck was as good a place as any to begin the hunt.

       It was down an old logging road, far beyond the dead end of a dirt road that branched off from an unmaintained paved road where Tom finally put the truck in park and killed the engine. Luke had no idea where they were. He wasn't familiar with this end of the county, and he doubted Tom was either, despite the man's claims otherwise.

       For a while, the men walked through the underbrush and the clearings, over hills and through valleys, trying to ignore the misery of being out in the cold for hours. It was no easy feat for Luke, as the chilled night air began to penetrate the layers of clothing he wore. The coldness bit at his skin. It wouldn't be long until he'd be down-right chilled to the bone.

Conversation was sparse among the men since sucking in the wintry air burned their lungs. Talking as they walked would only make it worse. Especially for a man as large as Tom, who already had to stop every little bit to double over and wait for a coughing fit to pass. There wasn't enough oxygen in all of southeast Missouri to allow him to walk and talk at the same time.

Through fields, the men walked side by side, spreading out and allowing the beams of the three flashlights to illuminate a wider berth.

As they made their way over treacherous terrain, they fell in line and walked single file, with Tom leading the way and setting the pace, Roy behind him, and Luke bringing up the rear. It was one of those times, while the men walked one behind another, that Tom stopped suddenly and cried out, "Holy shit!"

Roy and Luke quickly stepped around the bigger man to see what had captured his attention. Their gazes fell to the ground at Tom's feet, where the beam of his light shone on yet another horrific sight. The second of the evening.

"Hot damn," Roy breathed. "Think the bigfoot did it?"

"Maybe," Tom said excitedly, eyeing the blood on the ground at his feet. The longer he studied it, the more animated he became. "We must be close."

Luke said, "Wait. We don't know that the animal we're looking for did that."

"How do you know it didn't?" Tom asked. "Why else would there be blood out here? And so damn much of it?"

"It's deer season. For all we know, some hunter killed and gutted a deer here."

"Oh yeah," Tom said, his excitement waning as he realized that Luke's explanation was most likely the real reason for the large pool of blood that stained the frozen earth in front of them.

Roy said, "But where are the guts?"

"Maybe an animal ate them," Luke guessed with a shrug.

Roy chimed in with, "Maybe the chabbacupra ate them."

Luke rolled his eyes and shook his head. "Hey, how often do you guys go to the bar?"

Tom said, "A few times a week."

Roy said with a grin, "Only on days ending with y."

"Well do me a favor," Luke said. "Next time you're going to the bar, drive past it, take a right at the stop sign, and go up to the library. Go inside. Read some books. Learn some words."

The men searched the ground, each thinking. Wondering.

Then Roy said, "You think a hunter left this too?" He aimed the beam of his flashlight at a print on the ground, frozen in a pool of blood. Tom and Luke stepped closer to investigate.

"I'll be damned," Luke said, bending over to better scrutinize the latest find.

Roy let out a cackle that hurt Luke's ears, and then he said, "I knew it!"

Luke knelt and placed his hand next to the partial print. "Holy shit," he muttered. "Hey, guys, look at the size of this thing."

Roy said, "This has to be the biggest bigfoot ever."

"Guess that means we're huntin' a biggestfoot," Tom said with a snicker.

The other men stood beside Luke, one on each side of him, looking down at the size of his hand compared to the size of the print embedded in the red muck.

"I didn't think bigfoots got that big," Roy said before finishing off his third beer. He crumpled the can and tossed it onto the ground, an act which would have normally launched Luke into a spiel about how horrible littering was and how Roy should be ashamed of himself for doing something so irresponsible and reckless. But tonight, there were far more important things to think about, and the discarded can escaped Luke's attention.

"Bigfoot isn't real, Roy," Luke said. His eyes scanned the entirety of the swath of blood. There was nothing other than the one partial print. Luke didn't think it looked like a human footprint at all, but if it was a human print, it would only be the heel. No toe marks. No arch. Nothing but a portion of the heel of whatever had walked through the blood. And whatever it was had to be massive to leave behind a print so big.

"Oh yes it is," Roy said. "My cousin Jimmy Don down in Arkansas has one living in his back yard."

Luke rolled his eyes and stood.

Tom asked, "No shit?"

"No shit," Roy said. "It steals his meat right off the barbecue grill in the summer."

"Really?" Luke asked, as if he believed Roy's outlandish tale.

"Yessirreebob."

"So it comes to his house pretty regularly?"

"All the time. I told him he ought to charge the damn thing rent." Roy cackled.

Luke said, "So I take it he has plenty of pictures and videos of it I can see to prove to me that it's real." He folded his arms across his chest, watching the smile slide off Roy's face and waiting for him to reply.

"No, I don't think he has any."

"So your cousin Jimmy Don has a sasquatch living in his back yard, coming to his house all the time, and yet he has no proof whatsoever to back up his claims. No pictures. No videos. Nothing. Why do you reckon that is, Roy?" Luke asked.

With a shrug, Roy said, "I don't know. I guess it's there so often, he figures he doesn't need any pictures. He can look at it any time he wants." The look on his face suggested Roy was proud of himself for coming up with such a slick answer.

But the roll of Luke's eyes said he wasn't impressed.

Changing the subject, Tom said, "I wonder why this thing is killin' people now. I mean, it's been eating well. Very well, in fact. It's been breakin' into people's homes and raiding their refrigerators. It's been tearin' through every garbage can in the county, rootin' for scraps. And if what I heard is true, it's eaten more than a few dogs and cats along the way. Not to mention the goats and cows. So if this thing's been eatin' so well, why is it killin' and eatin' kids now?"

Luke stared at Tom for a moment, thinking about what he had said. He made a good point. He then turned around, shining his light on the ground beyond the bloody patch. He saw a trail of snapped twigs and crushed leaves leading away from the pool of blood and disappearing into the forest.

Tom said, "Well, what are we waiting for? It left us a trail to follow. Let's go." He took a step forward but stopped when Roy spoke.

"Go where?"

"What do you mean 'go where?'" asked Tom, turning to face his friend. "To find the damn bigfoot. Where else?"

"But…" Roy looked from Tom to the massive partial print and back again.

"But what? Are you scared now that you saw one little ol' print?" Tom asked with a smile.

Pointing at the ground, his eyes growing wide, Roy said, "That's not a little ol' print. That damn thing is huge."

"Oh hell," Tom said with a wave of his hand. "That's nowhere near huge. You wanna see huge, I'll show you huge." He began to unfasten the crotch of his coveralls.

"Alright," Luke said. "Let's all keep our clothes on, shall we?"

Looking back at the print, Luke wondered what kind of animal could've left it.

Tom continued, "Come on, fellers. We're out here to find it, and it looks like we have. Or at least we're gettin' close to finding it. Don't chicken out on me now, Roy. Think of the money."

"All the money in the world won't do us a damn bit of good if we're bein' shit out by a bigfoot or a chobbacupra one piece at a time," Roy said.

Shaking his head, Tom replied, "Oh hell. It ain't gonna eat us."

Roy snapped back with, "Why do you say that, Tom? Because bigfoots don't eat people? Hello! It just ate a person this morning!"

"Well then," Tom said, "it's probably not hungry."

"That's not funny," Luke mumbled. He appreciated a good joke as much as anybody, but a little girl had died. He didn't find any humor in the situation.

"Alright then," Tom said, growing more solemn. "Look at it this way, Roy. No matter how big the bastard is, it can't eat all three of us at the same time, right? So if it starts to eat one of us, the other two can kill it and get away. And hey, big bonus for the two who live. They only have to split the money in half instead of in thirds. So really, it's a win-win situation. Except, I guess, for the person who gets eaten."

"Really?" Luke asked dryly. "That's your best argument?"

"It's all I can come up with, yeah. You got anything better?" Tom asked.

Before Luke had a chance to respond, Roy said, "You know, guys, I'm freezin' my balls off out here. I can't feel them *or* my toes. I say we just call it off and go home."

"But you wanted to search for the damn thing," Tom said. "You were as excited about it as me and Luke were."

Luke had never been excited about it, but he didn't correct Tom.

"That was before," said Roy. "Now I'm tired, I'm cold, and I'm a little bit buzzed."

No, Luke thought. Roy woke up buzzed. He was far beyond that now.

"Naw," Tom said, shaking his head. "I think you're a little bit scared." He grinned at Roy, the grin that he had shown so many times back when they were young boys and he was trying to talk Roy into doing something he didn't want to do. It was a grin that said *you're too chicken shit to do what I want you to do, and I'm going to tell everyone all about it later and the whole town will laugh at you and think you're a coward.* It was a routine that always worked. That grin had got Roy to climb the lookout tower in the park during a terrible thunderstorm while it swayed wildly back and forth in the fierce winds. It had got Roy to jump off the bluff at Cardareva and into the icy cold waters of Current River in the middle of January. There had been a wide variety of other dangerous things over the years that Tom had been able to persuade Roy to do, most of which ended with an injury of some sort. And the hijinks always started with that grin.

"So what if I am scared?" Roy asked. "What if I don't want to end up like that little girl, huh? What if I would rather go home and fight with the wife than tromp around in the woods until I get eaten by an oversized squatch with a tapeworm? Is that so wrong? Does wanting to live make me a wuss? Because if it does, then fine. I'm a wuss. I'm a chicken with feathers coming out of my ass. A yellow-bellied coward. But I'll tell you this," he said, holding up a bony finger. "I'm going to be a coward who lives." He was firm and defiant, something Tom had never seen in him before.

Shocked at his friend's outburst, Tom was struck speechless. He looked at Luke, the brightness of his headlamp forcing Luke to put a hand over his face to shield his eyes.

27

A tension fell between the two men, the air between them as thick as it was cold. Roy had finally stood up to Tom after decades of being tricked and bullied into doing things he didn't want to do. Tom, not used to such a thing, was unsure of how to react. Luke sensed this tension, and it made him uneasy.

To lighten the mood a bit, Luke said with a shrug, "I don't know if *that* makes you a wuss, but your haircut certainly does." For a few seconds, his words hung in the air. No one moved. No one spoke. Luke added, "And that fanny pack isn't helping your case any."

Suddenly, Tom burst into laughter that doubled him over and launched him into a coughing fit. Roy followed suit, laughing equally hard but without the lung spasms that racked the larger man of the group.

With the mood now lightened, Luke could relax. His nerves had been frayed, though. While his friends laughed, he took off his gloves and tucked them under his arm, pulled the can of tobacco from his pocket and pinched a wad of the black stuff between his index finger and thumb, and placed it in his mouth where he used his tongue to pack it between his cheek and gum. He felt better already.

When the laughter died down, Tom slapped Roy on the shoulder and said, "What the hell. I'll take you home, and me and the bloodhound here can come back out and find the damn thing ourselves. We won't split the money with you, but we'll buy you a beer. How's that sound?"

"Hey, at least I'll be alive to drink it," Roy said, happy that he could go home. He pulled a pack of cigarettes from his pocket, thumped one out, and lit it.

The men turned and went back the way they came, heading for the truck while chatting about how sorry Roy would be when they killed the beast and he didn't get any of the glory or the money. But both their trek to the truck and their conversation was soon cut short by a scream.

The smiles slid from their faces, and their eyes grew wide. All three men stopped moving, stopped breathing, and listened intently to the night around them. A minute passed. Then two. It wasn't until after three eerily silent minutes had gone by that any of them dared to speak.

"What the hell was that?" breathed Roy.

28

Shaking his head, Luke whispered, "I don't know."

Tom forced a fake laugh and said, "Oh hell, that was a coyote. Just a coyote. Nothin' more." He shrugged, trying to convince the other men—as well as himself—that what they'd just heard was normal. Just another ordinary sound of the Ozark wilderness.

"No," Roy said, shaking his head. "Coyotes don't sound like that. They yip. Like yappin' puppies. They don't scream like..."

"Like what?" Tom asked, curious to hear what Roy would say.

Roy looked from Tom to Luke, trying to swallow his fear and avoid saying what he really wanted to say.

Taking the pressure off him, Luke said, "Like a human. Coyotes don't scream like a human."

"They sure don't," Roy added, happy to know he wasn't the only one who believed that what they'd heard was a person screaming.

"There's no way that was a human," Tom said. It could've been the cold that made his voice quiver, but more likely it was his dread and the fear that Luke and Roy might be right.

That they most likely *were* right.

When Luke opened his mouth to speak, another shriek cut through the wintry night, erasing all doubts the men had as to whether or not the first scream had been that of a fellow human being.

chapter **FOUR**

Before the second scream wound down, the three men were already on the move, all heading in the same direction, their feet carrying them toward the sounds of some poor soul's agony.

If Luke had been asked on any other day whether he thought Roy and Tom were brave, his answer would've been a resounding no. While they were both nice guys who would do anything to help a friend and almost anything to help a stranger, neither of them had ever done anything even remotely brave. Roy would argue that the things Tom had tricked him into doing over the years were brave, but they weren't. They were stupid, and he was stupid for letting himself be manipulated into doing them. But if Luke were to be asked now, in the frigid November night as they moved rapidly and without hesitation through the tangled underbrush of the dark forest, rushing headlong toward trouble without hesitation, his answer would be vastly different. While he still didn't consider himself to be brave, he now thought of his friends that way.

Another scream came, short and shrill.

The men stopped in unison, listening closely to determine if they were still heading in the right direction.

Veering to the right to straighten their course, they continued rushing to the aid of whoever was in need of help.

Without stopping, Roy asked, "What do you suppose is goin' on?"

The brisk walk over uneven terrain had left Tom too winded to speak. He gasped for air and coughed, leaving Luke to answer the question.

"I don't know. Maybe he stepped in a trap. Or maybe he was shot by a hunter's stray bullet. Hard to say. It could be something as simple as he stepped in a hole and broke his ankle."

Another shriek, cut short this time, leaving the scream incomplete.

Roy said, "That sure doesn't sound like the wails of a man with a broken ankle."

"No it doesn't," Luke admitted. He didn't want to believe they were rushing toward danger, but he was starting to experience a strange feeling in the pit of his abdomen. The feeling of imminent doom. Of dread and fear. And somewhere, deep in the mixture of emotions, was a bit of regret.

He shouldn't have answered the phone.

A limb slapped against his cheek, leaving a welt that burned like fire. He grimaced but didn't slow his steps. He wanted to slow down. He wanted to stop running. Hell, he wanted to turn around and go back to the truck, lock the doors, and race back to his house where he could throw his arms around Susan and pretend this whole night never happened. But if there was someone in need of help—and there evidently was—he couldn't do that. He had a daughter at home and a god above that he would one day have to explain his actions to. He could either tell them that he tucked his tail between his legs and ran away, or he could say with pride that he did the right thing when it was required of him, that he jumped in and rose to the challenge. He had to set an example for his daughter, and he was determined that it would be a good one.

By the time the men reached a slight clearing in the woods, Tom had fallen behind considerably. His steps had slowed to the point of little more than a normal-paced walk, and his breathing was beginning to worry Luke. His gasps and coughs completely drowned out their footsteps, and the wheezing reminded Luke of a certain space war villain. If they went much further, the man might very well keel over and die.

When they reached the break in the trees, Luke and Roy stopped, giving Tom a chance to catch up. They stood just past the tree line and surveyed the area, their flashlights doing little to illuminate the vast expanse.

"How come my light isn't as bright as yours?" Roy asked Luke.

Glancing at the beam of Roy's headlamp, Luke replied, "Looks like your batteries are low. You should've replaced them before we left town."

"Figures," Roy muttered.

Behind them, Tom emerged from the trees, gasping and wheezing. He nearly collapsed onto the ground but managed to remain standing, though his legs wobbled, and his chest heaved. Bending over, Tom braced himself by resting his hands on his knees, which made it a little easier to catch his breath. "See anything?" he asked, barely looking up from the ground. He squeezed his eyes closed to fight off the blackness that circled the edges of his vision. It was something that had been happening a lot lately. Just like the tightness in his chest. He hadn't told anyone about either of these things yet, but he was starting to think that maybe he should.

"Nothing yet," Luke said.

"Wait. There. What's that?" asked Roy, squinting and pointing at something beyond the trees. He reached up and thumped on his headlamp, hoping to make the light brighter. Tapping on it did nothing to strengthen the glow.

Luke followed Roy's gaze, his eyes settling on movement through the trees. A large shadowy figure was hunched over, hunkering near the ground. Green eyes reflecting the light of Luke's headlamp.

"What the hell is that?" Luke asked, barely speaking above a whisper.

Shaking his head, Roy muttered, "I don't know. But I'm not takin' my eyes off it."

For a moment, they stared in silence, trying to make out the behemoth mass but having no luck.

"Think it's the bigfoot?" Roy asked.

"Of course not." Although, calling it a sasquatch was as good as anything else Luke could come up with.

"Is it a choppeecoppra?"

"No. Aren't Chupacabras supposed to be small? Like dogs?"

"Thought you didn't believe in 'em."

"I don't. That's why I said they're supposed to be. This thing's a hell of a lot bigger than a dog," Luke said, squinting in the hopes of making out some sort of detail on the hulk.

"Then it must be a bigfoot."

Luke would've stated once again that the mythical creature was just that—a mythical creature, but with his eyes on the thing, his mind began to think that maybe, just maybe, sasquatches were real, and he was looking at one.

"Is it the screamer?" Tom wheezed from behind them.

Luke shrugged, then realized that in the dark Tom most likely couldn't see his response, so he said, "We don't know." He studied the mass, which was hard to make out from such a distance and in so much darkness. There were light spots. Dark spots. Even darker spots. Some of it moved. Most of it didn't. "I don't know what the hell that is," Luke said quietly.

The words had barely left his mouth when another scream—this one garbled and wet—pierced the night, leaving no doubt that it was, in fact, the screaming man they'd been looking for.

This time when the scream stopped suddenly, the hair on the back of Luke's neck stood up. It was a primal warning, his instinct's way of telling him to stay alert and be wary.

"Something's wrong," Luke said as he took off running. As his legs pumped beneath him, he realized that he should've gone the other way. Toward the truck. Toward safety. Toward Susan and Hope. Instead, he ran further away from all those things and straight toward danger and the unknown.

He was either a hero or an idiot. It seemed there was a fine line between the two.

Roy followed suit, running a few steps behind Luke as they ran through the forest, around oaks and pines and briar bushes, the barbs snagging their clothing.

Tom stood up and muttered his disappointment at having to move again. "Ah, damn it." Then, he followed his friends, but he was nowhere near as fast as they were.

In that moment, Tom wished like hell he hadn't eaten all those burgers and fries and pizzas and tacos. And he probably shouldn't have drank all those beers either. It was a delicious medley of food and drink that had created far too much weight for one man to carry. It had seemed like such a good idea at the time, ordering seconds and thirds of the things he loved to shovel into his gullet. But now, not so much. The excess weight jiggled and shook, gravity pulling it down toward the earth with each step, causing his feet to hurt, his knees to ache, and his back to burn. He ignored all that and pushed on, knowing that whoever was at the other end of those screams was in far more pain than he was, and unlike Tom, the other man's pain wasn't of his own doing.

Meanwhile, Roy was making good strides. Especially for a man whose blood alcohol level was far beyond the legal limit for operating a motor vehicle. But then he stepped in a hole, his ankle twisting at an awkward angle. He stumbled and fell, not feeling the pain for a few blissful seconds. He went down hard, his chin hitting the frozen and unforgiving ground. His teeth clanked together, jarring his head and giving him an immediate headache.

Up ahead, Luke heard Roy fall, heard the grunt and groan escape him as he connected with the ground. He glanced over his shoulder to check on his friend. "Are you alright?" he called out, his steps slowing a bit.

"I'm good," Roy answered with another grunt, pushing himself up. He winced as he carefully put his weight on his injured ankle, testing it to see if it was broken. It hurt like hell, but nothing seemed to be broken or sprained. No doubt, it'd be sore for a few days, but it should be able to carry him through the night. He just needed to put a beer on it.

Luke picked up the pace again, racing toward the man in need of assistance. In his chest, his heart pounded furiously, and it wasn't just from the exertion of running. He was scared. Terrified even. Earlier, when he had listed the possible reasons for a man to be screaming this deep in the woods in the middle of the night, he had done so to reassure his friends as well as himself. But the truth of the matter was Luke knew that whatever they found wasn't going to be as straightforward as a man with a broken bone. The screams emanating from that person were so horrible, so horrendous, there was no way they came from a pain as simple as that. No, those sounds could only come from a man in the type of agony most people would never experience in their lifetime. If they were lucky, that is. He knew this deep down, just as Tom and Roy most likely knew it.

As he drew closer, Luke slowed to a jog, and then he stopped altogether, trying to process the scene before him.

The screaming man was on the ground, torn to shreds and covered with blood. Hovering above him, its teeth sunk deep into the man's flesh, was something Luke had never seen before, something he never expected to encounter. Yet there it was, not far from him, ripping a man to pieces.

It was a colossal creature of some sort. He couldn't see it well enough from this distance to make out any details, but from what he could tell, the thing didn't fit the profile of any of the animals known to live in the Ozarks. Or anywhere else, for that matter.

The fact that he didn't recognize it, couldn't even venture a guess as to what it was, left no doubt that it was the very thing they were looking for.

"Hey!" Luke shouted, shining his flashlight at the beast's head to get its attention.

The creature looked up at Luke, blood and spit sliding from between its teeth and oozing from its black lips in long strands. It worked its jaws, chewing intently on a piece of flesh that had been ruthlessly torn from whoever lay on the ground beneath it.

Luke had a hard time processing the scene. He was looking at an animal that had, for whatever reason, developed a taste for human flesh. The progression in its diet had been quick, going from garbage to animals to people in a matter of days. As he watched it tear the man apart, questions flooded his mind.

What was this thing?

Where did it come from?

Why was it here?

Why was it eating people?

And what were they going to do about it?

It seemed the only way to stop it would be to kill it. There was no doubt about that.

As Luke came to this realization, he also became aware of the fact that the only thing standing between him and this man-eater was fifty feet and a handful of trees. The thing could be on him in a second if it chose to be. And he stood there with only a flashlight.

"Roy," he said sternly but quietly, without taking his eyes off the monster. "Get your ass up here. Now."

He heard Roy's footsteps approaching, uneven and slower than before, and then he heard the man's rapid breathing. "I'm coming. I'm coming." He stopped alongside Luke, shocked at what was captured in the beam of Luke's flashlight. "Holy shit," he breathed. "Is that...? It has a snout."

"Yeah," Luke said.

"Guess that rules out bigfoot."

"Shoot it," Luke said.

"What?"

"Fucking shoot it," Luke demanded without raising his voice. He didn't want to break the trance-like state the beast seemed to be in. He was afraid that shouting would agitate it and cause it to charge at them, and that was the last thing he wanted to happen. "Shoot the damn thing, Roy. And don't shoot to maim. Shoot to kill. Got it?"

"What? Oh. Yeah. Okay." Roy fumbled with the rifle, pulling the sling off his shoulder and getting it tangled around his arm before bringing the gun up and placing the butt of the stock against his shoulder. He closed one eye, looked through the scope, and put the crosshairs on the thing's head. His breathing hadn't slowed yet and his heart was racing, causing the rifle to wobble in his arms, bobbing up and down, the crosshairs wavering all over the creature. "Fuck," he spat, willing himself to calm down and take a clean shot at the thing.

"Are you gonna shoot it or what?" Luke asked, irritated that it was taking his friend so long to pull the trigger.

"I can't...ah, damn it! I can't hold the damn thing still long enough to get a shot."

"Just shoot it."

"Where? The head? The chest? The ribs?"

"I don't give a shit where you shoot it, Roy. Just. Fucking. Shoot it. Now."

Feeling pressured to act, Roy squeezed the trigger, sending a .30-06 round flying directly toward the wild animal.

And right over its head.

"Fuck!" Roy shouted.

"Shoot it again," Luke yelled. It didn't matter if he raised his voice now. The trance had already been broken by the sound of the gunshot tearing through the quiet night and echoing off the hills around them. The animal stood up on its back legs, pawing the air with its front feet and roaring a guttural growl that set Luke's teeth on edge. "Roy!" he shouted, still not taking his eyes off the animal.

Beside him, Roy yelled back, "I'm trying!"

Luke looked away long enough to glance at Roy, to see him fumbling with the bolt, trying to load another round in the chamber.

"I can't get it," he said. "The damn thing's stuck!"

Luke took a step backward, watching the creature as he did so. He expected it to charge at him at any second. "Roy," he said, his voice even now.

"I'm trying," Roy said. Sensing that his friend was backing away from him, Roy said frantically, "Damn it, Luke! Don't you dare leave me. Don't you leave me here to die alone, god damn it."

"You won't die if you shoot it, Roy," Luke said, taking another step back.

The thing stopped roaring. Stopped pawing the air.

"Why is it so big?" Luke muttered to himself, horrified at the size of the massive beast.

Roy continued to fumble with the rifle's bolt, yanking and pulling on the thing, trying to unjam it.

Luke watched as the animal dropped down and planted all four of its huge feet—paws?—on the ground and began running toward them. He shouted, "Roy! Run!"

Roy looked up from the rifle, saw the beast charging, and gave up on trying to clear the jam. He adjusted his grip on the gun. He turned it around in his hands and held it like a baseball bat, gripping it by the barrel, ready to bludgeon the goliath with the wooden stock if it came to that. And clearly, it was about to come to that because the bastard was closing in on him.

Fast.

Roy stood his ground, ready to swing with all his might. He bent his knees and leaned forward, putting all his weight on the balls of his feet.

The creature grew closer, running between the trees, zigging and zagging rapidly and gracefully as it rushed toward them.

Fifteen feet away now.

Ten.

Then, it disappeared. One second, it was there. The next, it was gone. But not really gone. It was still there. Somewhere. They could hear it. They could smell it. They could feel its eyes on them. But it moved so quickly and so nimbly, they couldn't keep track of it. It was in front of them, and then it wasn't.

Suddenly, the beast lunged from Luke's left with the agility of a cat and the weight of an elephant, knocking him out of the way as it hurled itself toward Roy.

Luke fell to the ground, his headlamp landing several feet away.

Roy watched in horror, frozen in place, and had just enough time to mutter, "Oh shit," before a shot rang out, reverberating off the hills and winding through the valleys.

The creature growled and dropped to the ground less than five feet away from where Roy stood. As soon as it went down, it sprang back up and took off again. This time, running away from the men instead of toward them.

Luke and Roy watched it disappear into the woods before looking at each other. They exhaled a breath they hadn't realized they were holding as Tom walked up behind them, wheezing.

"The next time I go fishin'," Tom said, "I'll be sure to bring you two clowns along. You make great bait."

"Fuck you," Roy said, clearly rattled.

"Tell me somethin', Roy. What's the sense in havin' a gun if you ain't gonna shoot the damn thing when we find it?" Tom asked.

"It jammed," Roy said, holding the rifle up as proof.

"Yeah? Well what about the shot you fired? What was that— a warning shot? Because you sure as shit didn't hit anything with it."

"Go to hell, Tom. At least I was up here and shot at it. Where were you?"

"I was back there watchin' the shit show. And you should thank me for bringin' up the rear. Otherwise, you'd be layin' over there next to that guy."

Tom's words reminded them that there was a dead man near-by. The joking stopped, and the gravity and seriousness of the situation returned full-force. The monster had taken another life. They had failed in their mission to prevent this very thing from happening.

It could never be said, though, that they hadn't tried.

chapter **FIVE**

Tendrils of steam rose from the many gashes in the dead man's body. Luke, Tom, and Roy all knew it was the body's internal warmth meeting the cold night air that created the smoke-like vapor, but each of them couldn't help but think of it as his soul departing this plane of existence and making its way on to the next.

As the men stood around the ogre's latest victim, looking down at what was left of him, Luke silently said a prayer for him and for his family, whoever they may be.

"What do you reckon we ought to do with him?" Roy asked, lighting another cigarette.

"I think you mean what do we do with what's left of him," Tom said dryly.

"*We* aren't going to do anything with him," Luke said. "That's not our job, and it's certainly not our place. We're going to call the cops. They'll call the coroner and alert the family." He pulled his cell phone from his pocket. As the screen lit up, he said, "Shit. Do either of you guys have a signal?" Luke returned his phone to his pocket while the other two men checked theirs.

"I ain't got shit," Roy said. "Damn thing ain't much more than a paperweight out here in the hills."

Tom added, "I've got one bar. I think." He brought the phone to his face, an older model flip phone, and squinted at the tiny screen. "Yeah. One bar. Shit. That's like when an ol' gal tells you to just use the tip. That ain't enough to do anything for anybody." He closed the phone and dropped it in his pocket. "Technology sucks out here in the sticks. And that's where you need it the most. Sonsabitches."

Sighing, Luke said, "Well, I guess we should walk to the top of a hill. Maybe we can get a signal there and call for help."

The men exchanged glances before Roy asked, "Then what?"

Luke replied, "What do you mean?"

"I mean what then? I assume we wait here for the cops, but then what'll we do? Go home? Keep trackin' the bigfoot that's not a bigfoot? What?"

Luke shrugged and shook his head. "I guess we need to find it." He nodded at the dead man lying on the ground. "If we don't, you can expect to see plenty more of this."

"Damn right," Tom said. "It's got a taste of human flesh. There ain't no goin' back from that. Berries ain't shit after you've had meat."

With a sigh, Roy mumbled, "I was afraid you were going to say that."

"Roy, we have to find it," Luke reasoned with him. "You know as well as I do that if we call it a night and go home, that thing will kill again. And again. How would you feel if you woke up in the morning and found out that someone you know, maybe your niece or nephew, had been killed by that thing? Could you live with that? Could you live with yourself, knowing that you could've prevented it? Because I sure as hell couldn't. I want to go home. I'm sure Tom wants to go home too. But as long as that thing is out here, roaming around and looking for trouble, we can't leave. We have to stay out here until we kill it."

Roy hesitated, then nodded, reluctantly agreeing. He knew Luke was right. He just didn't want him to be. He had thought he was ready to face anything, especially with the liquor and the adrenaline coursing through his veins. But in the heat of things, when he stood face-to-face with it, Roy realized that he wasn't anywhere near as tough or as ready as he thought he was. Now, he felt like a fool. Maybe Tom was right. Maybe he was a wuss.

"And by the way," Luke said, "I think it's safe to say that thing is not a bigfoot."

Roy looked at Luke, then at Tom. He looked down at his shoes and nodded slightly.

"What do you think it is?" Tom asked.

Luke shook his head. "I have no idea. I didn't get a very good look at it. It knocked me down trying to get to Roy. My head-lamp fell off." To Roy, he asked, "Did you get a good look at it as it came at you?"

Shaking his head, looking slightly shell-shocked, Roy said, "My batteries are dyin'. That thing was as dark as the rest of the for-est, so I couldn't see much. Just…hair. Lots of dark hair. And teeth. Long. Sharp. And a lot of them. Pieces of stuff stuck between them. Dark, bloody lips…" He stared at the ground, traumatized at nearly being mauled by whatever the hell that thing was.

A few seconds of silence passed, then Luke said, "Thanks, Picasso, for painting such a pretty picture for us."

Tom laughed, then slapped his hands together and said, "Okay then. How do we figure out who's walkin' to the top of the hill? Should we draw sticks or measure peckers or what? Because I've got to say, if we measure peckers, one of you two are gonna be walking."

"Whatever," Roy said, trying to forget about his near-death experience. Then he and Tom spent a couple of minutes trading jabs back and forth about who was better endowed.

Luke tuned them out and thought about who should go. He knew that Roy was afraid, not to mention well on his way to being blackout drunk, so he wouldn't ask him to go off on his own. He also knew that Tom was having a hard time breathing and trekking through the woods, so he didn't want to make him do any more walking than he had to. It seemed the only logical thing to do was volunteer himself for the job.

"I'll go," he said, cutting their juvenile conversation short.

Roy grinned, his body relaxing with relief, which he didn't even bother trying to hide.

With a smile, Tom said, "Alright then. Me and Roy will keep hunting."

"Wait, what?" Roy said, the grin disappearing as he tensed again. His eyes widened, his eyebrows raised. He said to Tom, "I'm gonna do what now?"

Surprised at the outburst, Tom was struck speechless for a moment. Then, he explained his way of thinking to his frightened friend. "There's no sense in us standin' around with our thumbs up each other's asses till either the cops come or we do. We'll just be wastin' valuable time. That thing was just here a minute ago. We can catch it if we go now. It doesn't take three people to make a phone call. Luke can make the call and wait for the cops. When they show up, he can lead them back here. In the meantime, we'll go get this sucker."

"But..." Roy struggled to find the words he needed. Words that would convey how much he wanted to go home without making him look like a coward. He didn't want to go anywhere near that behemoth again. Especially not so soon after being damn near killed by it. "But what about him?" He pointed to the dead man.

"What about him?" Tom asked, confused as to what Roy's point might be.

"Shouldn't we stay with him? You know, until the cops come?"

Tom laughed. It was too loud and entirely out of place in the forest, standing next to what was left of a bloody corpse. But he did it all the same. When he was finished, he asked Roy, "What good would it do to stay with him? He can't get any more dead than he is right now. And he certainly isn't goin' anywhere."

Luke thought it felt wrong and seemed disrespectful for Tom to say such a thing about a deceased person. Especially while the warm blood was still oozing from his many wounds. But he said nothing. Maybe that was just how the man dealt with something so traumatic. Dark humor.

Luke looked down at the man, wondering who he was. Reynolds County was 814 square miles and contained barely 6,000 people. In an area that small, he was bound to know the guy.

"Okay," Luke said, mostly to stop Tom from saying anything else disrespectful to the dead. "What do you want to do, Roy? Do you want to go make the call and wait for the cops while I go with Tom to find the...whatever the hell that thing is?"

Almost immediately, Roy nodded his head emphatically and said yes. He didn't think about what that option would mean, didn't comprehend that he would be all alone in the woods until the police arrived. Which, in this area, could take forever. He simply jumped at the chance to not have to chase after a wild animal with a thirst for blood that couldn't be explained or quenched.

"Fine. Give me your gun." Luke held his hand out, fully expecting Roy to hand it over.

"What? Why? No. I'm not givin' you my gun. Are you crazy?"

"Look, I'm the one going after that thing. I need the gun. You're making a phone call. You just need a phone. Now give it to me."

"No way. Tom has a gun. Let him do the shooting." When Luke continued to hold out his hand, Roy added, "Besides, my gun jammed, remember? It was Tom who saved your ass. So you don't need my gun. You need Tom. And you have Tom."

Seeing that Roy had no intentions of relinquishing his weapon, Luke dropped his arm and sighed. He shook his head and said, "Fine. Whatever. But if I die, I hope you feel like an ass for the rest of your life about this."

"That's a chance I'm willin' to take," Roy said, tightening his grip on his rifle.

"Be sure you tell that to Susan at my funeral. Let's go," Luke said, turning and walking past Tom. Away from Roy. Away from the remains of the last person who had fought the monster and lost.

Tom's footsteps were heavy, his breathing even heavier. Luke couldn't believe that Roy expected him to count on this guy to save his life. The guy who weighed as much as two Lukes and half a Roy. The guy who could barely breathe standing still on flat ground, much less walking up and down these steep hills. But it was what it was. He would just have to make do with what he had.

"Wait," Roy shouted.

Luke and Tom stopped and turned, watching as Roy jogged toward them.

"Here." Roy held the gun out for Luke to take.

"You sure?"

"Yeah. Take it."

43

"What made you change your mind?" Luke asked, reaching out and taking the rifle.

With a shrug, Roy said, "The thought of you dyin' because of me. I don't want that on my conscience forever. Frankly, I'd rather go up against a crazed bigfoot than an angry Susan. I feel I'd stand a better chance of survivin' the bigfoot. Besides, you're right. You're going after that thing. You need the gun. I'm goin' to make a phone call. I just need a phone. And I've got a phone." He patted his pocket and grinned.

Luke smiled and nodded. He worked the bolt, making sure the jam was clear. Then he looked at Roy and said, "Thank you. I take back all the bad things I've ever said about you. Well, most of them. Some of them were true, and I stand by those."

Roy chuckled. "Just go and kill the damn thing so we can go home, will ya?"

"That's the plan," Luke said.

Roy handed Luke extra ammunition, which Luke dropped into the front right pocket of his pants. He felt the cold brass against his leg, felt the added weight pulling on that side of him.

Then the men parted ways, each setting off to perform their assigned tasks. Each terrified of the night that lay ahead.

chapter **SIX**

It felt as if Roy had been walking for miles, and it was very possible that he had been. It was easy to lose track of where you were in the dense forest, especially at night, with nothing more than a headlamp that held dying batteries to lead the way. Plus, he was focused more on finding a strong cell signal than he was on paying attention to where he was going. That's why he had already tripped over a log and three tree roots and had been slapped in the face with more low-hanging tree branches than he cared to count. It was also why he wasn't entirely sure of where he was now.

Finally, with his injured ankle throbbing in time with the pounding in his head, he decided to stop and rest and get his bearings. So far, his phone had only been able to attain two bars out of five. He knew from experience that trying to make a call with anything less than three bars would be futile. He had to keep looking for that sweet spot, for a point on a hill high enough and clear enough of tree canopies to allow him the extra boost he needed.

"This damn county needs more towers," he said aloud, comforted by the sound of his own voice. "One damn tower for the whole county. Ridiculous." He had gone on more than a couple of rants about the subject over the years, and he would no doubt go on plenty more in the future. Those tirades hadn't changed a thing, of course. There was still only one cell tower servicing the entire county. A single tower to cover more than 800 square miles. It was absurd. And it was why the northern part of the county had no service at all. If it did, he might not be traipsing around in the dark, hoping to find a hill tall enough to afford him a signal. Then again, even if he climbed to the top of the tallest tree on the highest mountain in the whole county, he might still be shit out of luck. That's just the way it was out in the boonies.

Roy looked around and found a fallen tree to sit on and rest. He couldn't stay still for very long, but he needed a minute—maybe two—to get off his feet. He needed to catch his breath and rest his aching ankle. He was getting too old for this kind of thing. It was becoming crystal clear to him why the older guys didn't hunt in the hilly areas, and if they did, they used ATVs to move around instead of depending on their legs and feet.

He sat smoking a cigarette, drinking the last of the two beers from his fanny pack, and sniffling, the cold air making his nose run. He studied his surroundings, trying to decide which way he should go next.

It wasn't lost on Roy that he was going to have a great measure of difficulty leading the cops to the dead guy. After all, he wasn't entirely sure where he was. And without knowing where he was, finding his way back to where he'd been would most likely prove to be a fool's errand.

He was starting to think that perhaps Luke should've been the one to call for help after all. Tom had already proven that he could handle the creature, so Roy would've probably been better off going with him, no matter how scared he was. But he had made his choice, and now he had to live with it.

Roy chugged the last of the beer and tossed the can aside. He took the last drag from his cigarette and flicked the butt to the ground.

The buzz he'd got earlier from the beers had long since worn off, most likely scrubbed away in an instant by the burst of adrenaline that came from almost dying in a freak animal attack. He was going to need more beer to help calm his frayed nerves.

A minute passed.

Then another.

"Screw it," Roy said, standing. "If I'm going to walk all over hell's half acre, then I might as well walk back to the truck for another beer. Or two. Or three." He chuckled at his own joke, though it wasn't funny. But when a twig snapped behind him, his smile disappeared.

He turned quickly, shining his light in the direction from which the sound came.

It could have been a squirrel.

"Tom?"

It could have been a deer.

"Luke?"

It could have been an elk. The Department of Conservation had brought in a herd a few years ago. It was the first time elk had been in the state of Missouri since the 1800s. There were over a hundred of them now, and more were born into the herd every year. He'd seen them himself a few times, and there had been reported sightings all over the county, so it wasn't outside the realm of possibilities that he would encounter one now. Although...now that he thought about it, they always went back to Peck Ranch in the fall for mating. It was home to them, the place where they lived until the Conservation Department released them into the wild. Running into one at this end of the county at this time of year was highly unlikely.

So if it wasn't an elk...

"Guys?"

It might have been a turkey, but the chances of that were next to none. Turkeys flew up to roost in the trees at dusk, and they didn't fly down again until dawn.

"Is that you?"

The only other thing that could have snapped a twig like that was a sasquatch, but they'd already ruled that out. Bigfoot didn't have a snout. Their faces were similar to those of a human. They weren't looking for a squatch, though Roy still believed they roamed these woods.

Roy felt his stomach clench, felt his throat tighten. He also felt his bladder and bowels threaten to let loose.

"Guys? This shit ain't funny," he said, trying to sound brave—which he wasn't—and calm—which he also wasn't.

He looked left and right, scanning the immediate area around him which his dim light barely illuminated, and muttered, "Armadillo. Maybe a possum. Squirrels make a lot of noise."

After a minute passed and he didn't hear anything else, he decided—or rather talked himself into believing—it was just a little animal, hopefully a friendly one, and it was most likely long gone by now, or at least completely uninterested in him. Roy turned back around and headed for the truck once more, trying to pretend that nothing had just happened. And really, nothing had happened. A twig snapped in the forest. Not exactly headline news.

"Oh, Roy," he said to hear himself speak. "You're paranoid. And you know what they say about being paranoid. Put a beer on it."

That wasn't a saying, but it should have been.

He moved quicker than before, talking to himself as he walked, which was the adult version of pulling the blanket over his head. It wouldn't do a damn thing to save him when the monster came, but it would certainly make him feel better until then.

chapter **SEVEN**

"Think he'll be okay by himself?" Luke asked, leading Tom through the forest at a pace much slower than he would've preferred. They started out walking faster, but Luke quickly discovered that the oversized man couldn't keep up with him and was therefore forced to slow down.

Way down.

"Sure he will. He's just goin' to make a phone call. It's us you should worry about. Did you see what that thing did to that guy back there? It obliterated him. That guy woke up this morning, probably took a shit, got dressed, left the house, and never once thought that it would be the last time he did any of it. Now he's layin' out here in the woods looking like a pile of ground beef."

"Jesus, Tom."

"Well he is," he proclaimed. "And to think that a little girl went through that same thing this mornin'...I sure hope she didn't look like that. I'd hate that for her parents. Can you imagine findin' your little girl like that?"

Luke shuddered at the thought of the creature mauling the girl and leaving her in the same state it had left the grown man. The horror her parents must have felt. The agony. It would be horrific enough to know what had happened to your daughter, but to see it happen, to see the aftermath. To have that awful image ingrained on your mind for the rest of your life, taking the place of all the good memories you had of your baby girl…The ones where she smiled. Where she laughed. The ones in which she grabbed your hand and pulled you along to show you something she'd done and was proud of. The memories of you kissing her goodnight. All wiped away, replaced with the horrific images of her torn to pieces and swathed in her own blood.

Unable to stand the images swirling through his mind, Luke changed the subject by asking, "So how's your dad?"

"Oh, he's doin' alright, I reckon. He has a weird flutter in his chest sometimes. I told him he better get it checked out, but you know how he is. Stubborn as a doggone mule."

"I see where you get it," Luke said with a smile.

"Hell, I got that from both sides. I used to spend a lot of time tryin' to figure out who was the most stubborn. Mom or Dad. Finally, I just gave up and decided they were both pigheaded." He laughed. "Guess I never stood a chance."

That conversation died down, which allowed Luke's mind to return to what he'd been thinking about before. After a while, he asked, "Do you think you shot that thing back there?"

Tom thought for a moment and answered, "I believe so. It dropped, didn't it?"

"Yeah, but then it got back up."

"But it dropped. That means I shot it."

"Yeah, but…"

"But what? I shot it. It dropped. It only got up again because I didn't hit it with a big enough round. I would've had to put a few slugs in it for it to stay down, given the size of the thing."

"Well I was just thinking that you said you shot that deer too, yet it took off on you."

"What are you tryin' to say, Whistlepig?"

"Nothing, I guess. I mean…How long has it been since you sighted in your gun?"

Tom tried to recall. "Hell, I don't remember. It's always been pretty accurate though."

"But if it's not lined up, that explains a lot. It explains why the deer got away and why that animal, whatever the hell it is, got back up."

"I'm tellin' you, I shot that thing, and I shot that deer too. Me and Roy followed the blood trail until we lost it."

"What about the monster's blood trail?"

"I didn't see one," Tom said.

"Exactly. If you hit it, wouldn't there have been blood?"

Tom thought for a moment. Then, "What difference does it make whether or not I shot it, anyway?"

"A big difference. If it's wounded, it'll be easier to deal with. Easier to find, too. We can just track the blood. It'll also be easier to kill because it'll be weaker the next time we come across it."

Tom responded with, "Hm."

The tip of Luke's right foot caught on a tree root that protruded from the ground. He stumbled but maintained his balance.

"You alright there, Whistlepig?"

"Yeah. I'm fine."

"I thought—"

Before Tom could finish his sentence, a sound broke the calm of the night. Both men stopped, listening intently. They turned their heads, shining their lights into the darkness.

Half a minute after the sound stopped, Tom whispered, "What the hell was that?"

Shaking his head, Luke replied, "I don't know. It sounded...it sounded sort of like a mountain lion, but..."

"But more like a monster?"

Luke nodded. There was no other way to explain it, so he said, "Yeah."

"It sounded far."

Not far enough, Luke thought. But then he remembered that he was in pursuit of the strange animal. He had to follow that sound, no matter how cold it made his blood run.

"Which direction would you say that came from, Tom?"

"That way," he replied, pointing to their left.

"That's what I thought too. Alright," he said, sighing. "Let's go." Luke took off, veering left and wishing more and more with each step that he had stayed home.

chapter **EIGHT**

After finally finding his way back to the vehicle, Roy fished a beer out of the cooler in the bed of the truck, popped the top, and downed it. He burped, crushed the can, and tossed it into the bed along with all the rest of the empty cans and bottles Tom never bothered to throw away.

He checked his cell phone, saw that he still only had two bars, and said, "Shit. Fuckin' Reynolds County." He wasn't sure what he would do if he was never able to attain a signal. They hadn't talked about it. He supposed if it came to that, he'd have to walk to the nearest house and ask to use their landline. The problem with that was he wasn't familiar with this part of the county and had no idea where the nearest house was.

Roy let down the tailgate and climbed into the bed of the truck. This was his last option. He made his way onto the roof of the cab and stood up carefully, holding each of his arms straight out to the side like an airplane in order to maintain his balance. When he felt steady on his feet, he checked his phone again. This time, it was there. That beautiful little line, the middle in a row of five. The magical third bar.

He dialed the numbers and pressed the phone to the side of his face. A few seconds passed with nothing but silence in his ear. Just as he began to think nothing would happen, the phone in the Sheriff's Office over in Centerville began to ring. When the dispatcher answered, Roy told her who he was, what had happened, and his best guess as to where he was and how the deputies could get to him. The connection was fuzzy, requiring Roy to repeat himself numerous times to be heard, but he successfully completed the call. When it was over, he returned the phone to his pocket and got back down into the bed of the truck, where he pulled two more beers from the cooler.

Roy sat on the tailgate and popped the top on one of the two cans of alcohol. He had done it. He managed to find the truck again and call for help. All was right in his world.

He wished he could say the same for the poor bastard that lay mangled in the woods, but he couldn't.

With the can of beer in his hand, Roy raised his arm, toasting the dead guy. "To you," he said toward the woods. "Whoever you are." He then drank from the can, relishing the taste of the sweet barley and hops.

He lit a cigarette and wondered what the guy's wife would say when she learned that he was dead. Then, he wondered what his own wife would say if it had been him instead. She might be sad at first. Maybe. But then she would most likely be grateful. Roy hadn't been the greatest husband to her, and he knew that. Hell, everybody knew it. But he was too damn old now to be any different than he was.

He had always been a messy guy. Dirty clothes on the floor of the bedroom. Wet towels on the bathroom floor. Whiskers in the bathroom sink. Piss on the toilet seat. Toenail clippings embedded in the fibers of the carpet. Food stains on the front of every shirt he owned. It wasn't so much that he was lazy, but more that he didn't mind the messes. And he figured if he didn't mind them, she shouldn't mind them either.

But apparently, she did.

There were things about her that Roy didn't like, but he didn't bitch and nag her about them the way she did him. For instance, she chewed with her mouth open. She licked her thumb before turning the pages of a book or magazine, making a slurping noise as she did so. She watched soap operas and talked about the characters as if they were real people. She read romance novels and liked to tell Roy all about the story as she read it and then again when she was finished. He hated all of those things and more. But he kept his mouth shut about them. In his mind, that was marriage. Keeping your mouth shut about all the things you hated about the other person in order to keep the peace. If you could manage to do that until one of you died, you'd had a successful marriage.

He supposed their life together hadn't been that bad. Not in the grand scheme of things anyway. They'd had far more than their fair share of rough times and arguments throughout the years, but they had also shared plenty of good times and laughs too. Though Roy was always a bit clueless when it came to things like relationships and feelings and all the other sentimental, mushy stuff that women seemed to crave, he had noticed that things had been vastly different since Linda had caught him in the lie. Not *a* lie. *The* lie. It certainly wasn't the only one he had ever told her, but it was the only one she had ever caught him in. And she had not forgot it, nor had she let him forget it. He didn't imagine that she ever would.

The girl had been nineteen years old, almost twenty when he had met her at the bar a few years back. Her name was Destiny. She was far too thin, all bones and no curves, which is the exact opposite of what Roy liked in a woman. But she had flirted with him and made him feel good. Not old. Not like a failure. When he was with her, he felt like a teenager again, without a care or a responsibility in the world. And yet at the same time, he felt like a real man. He was older and wiser than her, so when he knew something she didn't—which was damn near always—her reaction made him feel smart. When she didn't have the money for something—again, always—he'd buy it for her, and her eyes would light up as if he'd just given her the world. She looked at him like a god, and he had let it go straight to his head. That quickly led to a physical affair, and as with everything else in their relationship, his experience—which didn't amount to much—made her think even more of him. He knew and could do things that boys her own age had never even heard of or had a clue how to do. Roy's head swelled even more after that. He became cocky and arrogant. He felt untouchable. And that's when he began to get sloppy in keeping it all hidden from his wife.

That was the problem with feeling that way. Once you started feeling like you were untouchable, you started to act like it. And as Roy had learned the hard way, no one was untouchable. Least of all him.

Once Linda found out about Destiny, she made him break things off with her, which was fine by him. That girl wore him out. She was full of energy and insatiable, and he was much too old to try to keep up with someone like that.

He never missed the girl, just the way she made him feel. That feeling of being a god, of being smart and successful and good. That feeling of being a real man. With her gone, he was back to being boring old Roy Johnston with the yellow teeth and the gaunt face and the job at the mill and the decades-old mobile home with the leaky roof and the rusty truck that rolled off the assembly line during the Reagan years. His life was shit, but for a brief period of time, he'd been able to forget all that with the help of Destiny. That was what he missed.

Roy crushed the empty beer can, the second of the two he'd sat down with, and belched. He sighed deeply and decided to call his wife. He tried to tell himself that he had simply lied to her about Destiny, but he knew deep down that it was more than that. He had cheated on her. He had hurt her, and he truly was sorry that he had.

While the affair with a teenage girl had made him feel good about himself, it had made Linda feel terrible about herself. She couldn't compare with youth, and she knew it. That hadn't stopped her from trying, though. After she found out about Destiny, she'd started to wear make-up and revealing clothing, something she'd never done before. She kept the house cleaner and cooked better meals. She tried to be what she thought her husband wanted and needed, and though he hadn't responded to her efforts, they hadn't gone unnoticed.

Unappreciated, yes. But not unnoticed.

He was an asshole. A selfish prick. He had never felt more like a rotten piece of shit than he did at that moment. Maybe it was the beers he had drank, or perhaps it was the silence and stillness of the forest which gave him a chance to reflect on things. More likely, it was coming face to face with the monster and thinking he was going to die that had brought up such dark thoughts and deep emotions. Whatever the case, he felt horrible.

Roy got up, farted loudly, and made his way once more through the rubbish in the bed of the truck to the cab, where he climbed on top of it and took out his cell phone again.

Linda answered, sounding as if she had been asleep. Roy wasn't sure of the time, so it was quite possible that she had already turned in for the night.

"Hey, baby," he said sweetly. "It's me."

"Roy? What time is it?" she asked, her voice heavy with sleep. "Where are you?"

"I'm not sure of either, to be honest with you. I just...me and the boys are out here—"

"The boys?" she asked, the sleepiness wearing off now.

"Yeah. Tom and Luke and me. We—"

"Did you find the deer yet?"

"Well that's the thing. See we *were* gonna go lookin' for Tom's deer, but instead—"

"Instead what?" Before he had a chance to respond, Linda snapped, "Roy, you better not be at the bar. We've talked about this."

"Baby, listen. Baby, no. I'm not at the bar. I haven't gone to the bar. I promise."

"Then where are you?"

"If you'd let me explain, I'll tell you."

"Fine. But it better be good."

"It is. And it's not."

"What the hell does that mean?"

"See, we were gonna go lookin' for that deer Tom shot, but after we picked up Luke, we stopped at the station to grab some snacks. That's when Tom told us that he'd overhead some guys talkin' about goin' huntin'."

"Hunting? There's no hunting after dark in Missouri. Have you left the state? Roy, if you've left the state, so help me god—"

"No, baby. Listen. You know that animal that's been causin' all that ruckus lately over by Lesterville and everywhere else? Well it killed a little girl this mornin' and—"

"It what? Oh my god. It killed a little girl? Who? Whose little girl?"

"I don't know. Um…" Roy said, squeezing his eyes shut and trying to recall the name he'd seen on the side of the mailbox at the scene of the little girl's death. Black mailbox. Gold letters. It started with an R… "Ramshaw, I think."

"Oh my god," Linda said, as the pieces of her day fell into place. "That's why Brenda Ramshaw didn't come to work today. And that's what everyone was so upset about. Oh wow. I knew something bad had happened, but I didn't know what or to who. That's awful."

"Yeah. It is awful. So anyway, Tom said he heard those guys talkin' about the animal. The little girl's dad—"

"Paul."

"What?"

"Paul. That's his name. The little girl's dad. Paul Ramshaw."

Roy squeezed his eyes closed, trying to ignore his wife's annoying habit of interrupting him while he talked. It was something she did all the time. He hated it. But he tried to remain focused on the reason he had called her. "He's offering a twenty-five-thousand-dollar reward for the animal. Dead or alive. So we're out here lookin' for it, and—"

"Wait. What? You all went out looking for that thing? Are you crazy? It's already killed one person."

"Two."

"What? What do you mean two?"

"We found the thing. It was…it was eatin' a guy. Or what was left of him anyway. That critter sure did a number on him. Tom and Luke took off after the thing, and I came back to the truck to call the cops. I got to thinkin' about you and just wanted to call and tell you I love you." He expected her to melt, to turn to mush over his words. Maybe even profess her undying love and loyalty to him in return.

Instead of melting, she said, "You're alone? In the woods? With a man-eating animal? Roy, have you lost what little of your mind you have left?"

"Don't worry, baby. It went the opposite direction of the truck, which is where I am now. I'm okay. Everything is fine."

After a few seconds, Linda sighed and said, "Well at least you have your gun."

"Well…"

58

"What do you mean well, Roy? You do have your rifle, don't you?"

Roy said nothing. He knew that if he did, he would never hear the end of it. It would be like the time he let the truck run out of gas when they were out of town. Ten years had passed since then, but still, every time the needle on the gas gauge made it to the half-way mark, she hounded him about filling it up so they wouldn't have a repeat of the last time he was careless and they ended up stranded at the side of the road.

"Roy Johnston, you answer me this minute. Where is your rifle?"

He closed his eyes and gave in to defeat. "I gave it to Luke."

"You what?"

Her voice was shrill and loud, causing Roy to wince and pull the phone away from his ear. It turned out that he could hear her just as well with the device several inches away from his face as he could with the thing pressed firmly against his skull.

"I can't believe you, Roy. I cannot believe you would do something so stupid as to give your gun to Luke. You're hunting a friggin' monster for crying out loud, and now you have no weapon. What are you gonna do—"

"Baby, I'm not huntin' the thing. Not anymore. I'm just sittin' here at the truck waitin' for the cops to show up. Tom and Luke are huntin' the damn thing. Luke didn't have a gun, and I figured he needed it more than me since he was the one goin' after it. Just calm down." Those were the magic words that set the little missus off on a tangent about how telling her to calm down would never, ever in a trillion million years make her actually calm down and about how Roy was the stupidest man on the planet if he thought he was safe without a gun while that animal prowled the woods. Minutes went by with her screaming into the phone, minutes in which Roy wished he hadn't called her at all, rolled his eyes, and shook his head more times than he could count. She yelled for a while about how stupid Roy was to think that Luke's life was worth more than his, and then about how her mother had been right about him all along. Then, she delivered the coup de grace.

"I tell you what, Roy, it's times such as these, when you do stupid things like this, that I wish I would've just packed your bags and let that whore have you."

That was it for Roy. He no longer felt selfish or like an ass-hole about having the affair. In fact, he felt foolish for not having more affairs. Destiny had made him feel good, and that's something he hadn't felt since he married Linda. He liked to tell himself that their relationship was normal, but he realized in that moment that it wasn't. Linda berated him about everything every chance she got. He was stupid. He was dumb. He wasn't good looking. He was a worthless drunk. He was lazy. He didn't make enough money. He was good for nothing. She should've married someone else. The list went on and on.

He had begged for her forgiveness in the wake of the affair. He hadn't really cared whether or not she forgave him. He just didn't want her to leave him. Being with her was all he'd ever known. Un-like her, he had never been with anyone else. Sure, he had dated a few other girls when he was a teenager, but none of them had lasted more than a couple of dates, and he'd never had sex with any of them. Therefore, he had no other relationships to compare theirs to. He didn't know what other women were like. For all he knew, they were all like Linda. But they weren't. He knew that now. He knew it because Destiny hadn't been like Linda. She hadn't put him down every chance she got. She hadn't treated him like shit. She hadn't made him feel the awful way his wife made him feel.

It was then that it struck him what that strange feeling was, the feeling that he'd been harboring deep down for so long but could never quite put his finger on. He felt that he'd been cheated out of life. He could've had a normal relationship with a woman who treat-ed him better if only he hadn't settled for Linda. It was all her fault that everything had happened.

His cheeks flushed with anger.

"You know what?" Roy asked, feeling a new-found courage welling up inside him. "I wish you would've too. Destiny was better than you in every way. I think maybe I'll give her a call. See what she's been up to." Roy imagined his wife sitting on their bed with the lamp on, one arm crossed over her chest, the other holding the phone to her ear with a look of shock on her face. He imagined her face turning as red as her hair with rage and disbelief that her hus-band, a man she'd spent years degrading and demeaning and beating down, had finally found his backbone and with it, the courage to talk back to her.

60

Instead, Linda said, "Go ahead. Call her. Ask her what she's been doing. Or rather *who* she's been doing. I think you might be surprised."

Roy's smile slid off his face. What did she mean by that? "What do you mean by that?"

Linda giggled. "Oh, you mean you don't know?"

"Don't know what?"

"Well I suppose it doesn't matter. You can ask her about it when you call her. Then you can tell me all about it when you come home."

"If I come home," he snapped. Then he ended the call without giving her a chance to respond. He stood there holding the phone, wishing he'd been able to slam it down rather than simply pressing a button to the end the call. Still, he was proud of himself for finally having the guts to stand up to her. Yet he was confused about what she'd said and terrified of what it might mean.

chapter **NINE**

"You think we're gonna find this thing?" Tom asked, his breathing labored as he stepped over a fallen tree.

Luke pondered the question before replying, "I don't know. It's hard to say. I mean, we're close. Hell, we were standing face-to-face with the damn thing a while ago. So it's possible. But these woods are big, and that thing is fast." It was a hell of a lot faster than Tom, Luke thought, but he didn't say that part aloud. He had no interest in making his friend feel bad about himself.

"Well if we do find it again, and I believe we will, don't hesitate. Don't do what Roy did and blow the shot, either. Just aim and pull the trigger. We've got to get that damn thing taken care of. I just keep thinkin' about that poor bastard back there. All mangled. I don't want that to happen to anyone else. And I damn sure don't want it to happen to one of us. So don't hesitate. Got it?"

Looking around for any signs that the creature had come this way ahead of them, Luke said, "Got it."

While Luke was focused on the ground, searching for tracks, he overlooked a clue that the thing had been there.

"Look here," Tom said, the beam of his headlamp lighting up the area which had captured his interest. On the thin branch of a sapling hung a sprig of hair. "The son of a bitch has definitely been through here."

Luke watched as Tom plucked the clump of hairs from the branch and brought it up to his face. He studied it closely, then held it under his nose and sniffed it. Luke rolled his eyes. "What the hell are you doing?"

"Smellin' it."

"No shit. I can see that. *Why* are you smelling it?"

"I'm makin' sure it's from our animal and determinin' if it's fresh or not."

"And you can tell all that just by smelling it," Luke said, not bothering to hide his sarcastic tone.

"I sure can."

"Interesting. I've known you my whole life, and yet I wasn't aware you had in-depth knowledge of all things animal."

"Well, there's a lot you don't know about me, smart ass. For example, I enjoy doin' word searches, shoutin' out the wrong answers to game shows on TV, and the relaxin' sound of rain on the roof during a thunderstorm. I'm tellin' you, I'm more than just a pretty face."

"Uh-huh. So maybe, then, you can tell me just how it is that smelling that little wad of hair is going to tell you if it came from our animal. How do you know the difference between skunk hair and deer hair or squirrel hair? And how would you know if it's from tonight or last night or last week?"

Tom looked from the hair he held between his thick thumb and forefinger to Luke and then back to the hair. "I just do," he said simply.

"Well I guess that settles that," Luke said dryly. "Thanks for clearing that up for me. I feel as if I know enough to become an animalologist myself."

Tom chuckled and repeated the made-up word. "Animalologist."

Luke watched as Tom continued to study the hair, then he laughed and shook his head.

Tom said, "It's black, so that rules out deer, elk, groundhogs, and squirrels. It's too high off the ground to be a skunk or a hog. That doesn't leave much else. It's our animal alright."

Luke mulled over the man's answer, which seemed to make sense. Then he said, "Okay. But how do you know it's from tonight?"

"It still smells like our animal. Like a hundred musty, wet dogs. If this hair had been here very long, the wind would've taken most of the smell with it. Other animals might've been able to smell it, but not me."

Luke looked at his friend. "I'm impressed. It seems you're a hell of a lot smarter than I tell people you are."

Tom laughed and said, "And you're a hell of a lot better lookin' than I tell people you are." Having gained all the information he could from it, he dropped the tuft of hair, letting it fall to the forest floor. "Now let's go get this sucker."

The men walked, chatting periodically to break the monotony of the task. They mostly listened to the forest around them, analyzing and scrutinizing every crunch of leaves or snap of twigs they heard. They stopped often for Tom to launch into a coughing fit and to catch his breath. Luke planned to demand that he see a doctor when the hunt was over. There was no way the man was in good health. Normal people didn't wheeze that hard and cough that much from merely walking. His friend needed a diet and most likely a whole slew of medications if he wanted to be around much longer. This wasn't the time to talk about it though, so Luke didn't say a word to Tom about how worried he was. But he would have plenty to say to him later.

At one point, Tom stopped walking. Panting, he said, "I've gotta sit down for a minute." He found a tree stump in an area that had been logged sometime in the recent past. There were dead tree tops scattered around the clearing, as well as fallen trees that didn't meet the logging requirements and deep skidder tracks that had dried and hardened and became part of the landscape.

Luke located a fallen tree not far from Tom and sat down for a rest.

The sound of his friend struggling to breathe bothered him. He listened as long as he could stand it before deciding to drown out the sound of it by talking. "Do you have any idea where we are?"

Tom looked around, then replied through ragged breaths, "I think so. I think this used to be Kerr-McGee land."

"That doesn't help much. Everything around here used to be Kerr-McGee land."

"Yeah, but I'm pretty sure I know where we are. At least the vicinity of where we are."

"As long as we're not lost."

"We're not lost. Not totally anyway."

Luke nodded. Then the sound of Tom's wheezing rattled him, made him feel the sting of what losing his friend would feel like, and so he kept the conversation moving. "You think Roy's okay?"

Tom waved his hand. "That son of a bitch is fine. He'll always be fine. I don't know how the hell he does it, but he always manages to be okay. Now when he gets home to that wife of his, that'll be a different story. He may not be so fine then." He laughed loudly, which sent him into a fit of coughing that ended with him gagging and retching.

It was hard for Luke to watch, so he looked at the ground between his feet and tried not to hear it. When he found the sound too loud to ignore, he tried talking over it. "You still seeing that girl from Piedmont? What's her name—Sarah?"

Tom shook his head. "Sadie. And no, I ain't seen her in a while now."

"Really? What happened? She get tired of putting up with you?"

"Nah. It was too much work driving back and forth to see her."

"Driving was too much work, huh? You're taking lazy to a whole new level, buddy."

Tom smiled. "Eh. I guess what I meant was the relationship wasn't worth the drive."

"I can understand that." He couldn't, but he didn't know what else to say. Then he thought of something. "Well, don't worry. I'm sure you'll find somebody else to put up with you. If Roy can, you can."

The big man gave Luke a knowing grin and said, "I already have."

"Oh yeah? Anyone I know?"

Tom tried to laugh but it only made him cough harder. When he got it under control, he said, "You know *of* her."

Luke nodded, waiting for more information to come. When none did, he asked, "Are you going to tell me who it is?"

"I hadn't planned on it."

"Ah. I see. Then there's only one logical conclusion I can come to."

"What's that?"

"She's not real."

"She's real."

"Nope. I think you made her up." Luke placed a wad of chew in his mouth.

Tom smiled. "Oh, she's real, alright."

"Then why won't you tell me who it is?" An idea struck Luke just then. "Oh," he said. "I get it. She's ugly, huh? You don't want to tell me who it is because you're ashamed of her."

Shaking his head emphatically, Tom said, "No, she ain't ugly."

"She must be old then."

"No, she ain't old. Matter of fact, she's younger than me. A lot younger than me."

"You're not...I mean...She's over eighteen, right?"

"Oh hell yeah," Tom said quickly. "Jesus, Luke. What kind of guy do you take me for?"

"Sorry. I just...You're not giving me much to go on here."

"I'd tell you more, but I can't right now."

"Now see, that circles me back around and makes me think she's fake. And I'll be honest with you, Tom. I'm going to be awful damn disappointed if I find out that your imaginary girlfriend is so old and ugly, you're too ashamed to tell me about her."

Tom laughed then, a deep laugh that launched him into the worst coughing fit yet and killed the conservation.

When the coughing died down and Tom finally caught his breath, the silence returned to the forest. Luke wasn't sure what Tom was thinking, but he knew what was on his own mind.

Susan.

When she'd agreed to marry him more than twenty-five years earlier, she hadn't agreed to this—the chance of becoming a widow because her husband felt brave enough or stupid enough to chase an angry man-eating animal through the woods at night. He felt like an ass for doing it, for risking something so important. But when he thought about the little girl and the man lying out on the forest floor, he knew he had to keep going, and he knew that his wife would understand.

"Psst."

Luke jerked his head up. He looked at Tom, who was looking back at him.

"Is it gone?" someone whispered.

Luke stood, looking around for the person behind the voice. A man. But who? And where was he?

"Who's there?" Luke asked.

"Is it gone?" the voice asked again, this time choosing to speak in regular tones.

"If you mean the killer animal, yeah. It's gone," Luke replied, still looking around for the speaker.

"Good."

"Where are you?"

"Over here."

The snapping of limbs and rustling of dead leaves clued Luke in as to the location of the person. He looked to his right, shining his light into a downed tree top that was still covered in dead leaves that refused to let go of the lifeless limbs. He watched as a man emerged and made his way over to where Luke and Tom waited.

The man was dressed in camouflage, his military-style flashlight clipped to the strap of the backpack he was wearing. He advanced gracefully, stepping over roots and rocks and fallen limbs as if they weren't even there. Like a butch ballerina.

"Name's John," he said, extending his hand to first Luke and then Tom. "John Ramshaw. I live over in Bunker." He was young, early- to mid-twenties, and full of that youthful energy that both Luke and Tom used to have and wished like hell they still possessed. Luke had the feeling he knew the guy, like maybe he'd met him before.

"I'm Luke Davis, and he's Tom Wilkins. We live over in Ellington."

"Okay. Yeah," he said happily, as if he had heard of them both and was thrilled to finally meet them. "You guys out here huntin' that thing too?"

"Yeah. And we found it just a little while ago," Tom said.

John's eyes widened. "No shit? What happened? Did you get it?"

"If we got it," Tom said with an attitude, "why the hell would we still be out here traipsin' through the damn woods?"

The young man tensed.

Luke said, "Don't mind him. He's just mad because there aren't any vending machines out here." He shot Tom a look that told him to knock it off.

Tom waved his hand at Luke, dismissing his admonition.

John smiled and nodded, relaxing once again.

Luke continued, telling him about their encounter with the beast and about finding what was left of the poor bastard who'd found it first.

Then, John told the men his own story. "Did you guys hear about that little girl that was killed this morning?"

Both Luke and Tom said that they had.

With sadness in his voice, John said, "That was my niece. I was out huntin' all day. Didn't make it in until about six o'clock this evening. Soon as I found out what happened, I turned around and headed right back out. I've been out here all night. Hadn't seen or heard a thing until a little while ago. I was sittin' down on that stump there, the same one you're sittin' on now," he said to Tom, "when I felt something on the back of my neck. At first, I figured it was a spider or a tick. But it didn't feel like a spider or a tick, you know. Plus, it's too damn cold for spiders and ticks to be out. So I thought it must be the wind. But then I realized that there wasn't any wind. That's when I got that cold fear, you know. That tightening in your guts and that chill in your bones when you know somethin' just ain't right. I turned my head and looked over my shoulder. The damn thing was standin' right behind me. Breathin' on my neck." He shuddered. "I get chills just thinkin' about it."

"I bet," Luke said, trying to imagine having such an encounter with the thing and trying desperately to place where he knew the guy from. "We were heading out to find a deer Tom shot that got away. We stopped for gas and he overheard some guys talking, and we all decided to come out and look for this thing instead. We figured this was more important," Luke said solemnly, feeling sympathy for the young man and his family.

68

"We all?" John asked, looking from Luke to Tom.

"Me, Tom, and Roy. Roy went to call the police about the guy we found in the woods."

John nodded once, slowly. He stared at Luke, unblinking. "The police, huh?"

"Yeah. That is, if he could make the call. It's hard to find a signal out here."

John nodded. "You got that right. I've been tryin' to call my brother off and on all night. I wanted to keep him updated, you know. I don't want him worryin' about me. I didn't even tell him where I was goin'. I just left the house half-cocked and in a hurry. The last thing he needs right now is somethin' else to stress out about."

"Well, I wouldn't worry about it too much right now. I'm sure with all of us out here searchin', some of us are bound to get that bastard before morning," Tom assured him. "Just you wait. With that reward up and all, I'll bet half the damn county's out here in these woods lookin' for that thing."

"Reward?" John asked, clearly unaware that his brother had offered up money for the beast that killed his daughter.

"Didn't you know?" Tom asked.

"All I know is I pulled up to my brother's house, saw blood around the mailbox and the yard full of vehicles, and I ran inside to find out was goin' on. Everybody was huggin' each other and cryin'. I found Paul and asked what was goin' on. He was cryin' too." John paused, his voice cracking. "That's only about the third time in my whole life I've seen him cry. He said somethin' got her. I asked who. Then he told me it was Maddie. I asked if she was gonna be okay. He said no. Said she was gone." John wiped at his eyes and added, "I turned around and left. Got in my truck and drove straight out here to look for the son of a bitch. I didn't really expect to find it, but I couldn't just sit around the house cryin' and huggin' people. I've gotta do somethin'."

Luke nodded, knowing he would most likely do the same thing if he were in the boy's position.

"So he put up a reward, huh?"

Tom nodded, the beam of his headlamp bobbing up and down with the movement.

"How much?"

69

"Twenty-five grand," Tom answered.

John said nothing for a moment. Then, "Well I won't take it. I fully plan on killin' it, but I ain't doin' it for the money. They can use that to bury Maddie." His voice cracked again, and he looked away from the men, scanning the trees around them.

Hearing the way John had refused the reward made Luke feel bad about the things he had planned to do with it. He suddenly felt selfish. Here he was, planning on buying Hope a car or stuffing a bank account for her to go to college when the man who was offering the money no longer had a little girl do those things for. Money was nothing. Little girls were irreplaceable.

Luke looked at Tom and wondered if he was rethinking his use of the reward money. The look on his face suggested that he just might be.

"You say your friend called the cops?" John asked.

"He was going to if he could get a signal. You know how it is out in the woods around here," Luke said.

John nodded again. He seemed to get lost in thought for a bit before saying, "Well I ain't gonna catch the damn thing sittin' around here yakkin' at you fellas all night. I guess I better get movin'."

"You're more than welcome to come with us," Luke said quickly, hoping the young man would agree to stay with them. He said it out of guilt over the reward money, but also because he felt somewhat responsible for the young man. If he let the kid go off on his own and he ended up being another victim, Luke would never be able to forgive himself. "We'd be more than happy to have you along."

John considered the offer for a moment before answering. "Nah. I think our chances will be better if we split up, don't you?"

Luke thought about it and reluctantly agreed. "You're probably right. But be careful out there. Not only is there a wild blood-thirsty beast roaming around, but it's also deer season. There's no telling how many armed men are out here. And I can't guarantee you all of them are sober." He personally knew of one who wasn't, but he didn't tell that to John.

John nodded. "I'll be careful. You fellas do the same. It was nice meetin' you, and good luck to ya." He shook each of their hands again.

70

While Luke shook John's hand, he couldn't help but ask, "Have I met you before?"

John tilted his head and smiled. "No. I don't believe so." The smiled seemed odd to Luke. Out of place. Maybe it was because it didn't reach the man's eyes. There was something off about it, but Luke couldn't place exactly what that something was.

"Huh. That's weird. I could swear I've met you before."

"Maybe I just have one of those faces." John let go of Luke's hand and stepped back, his eyes never leaving Luke's.

"Maybe," Luke said. But he knew that wasn't it. He'd been studying John's face since the man had stepped out of the downed tree top, and he was certain that he'd never seen his face before. But still, there was something familiar about him.

Luke watched John walk away and hoped that the young man would be the one who brought the beast down, even though it would mean no reward money for him or Tom or Roy. No car for Hope. No padded bank account for college. But none of those things mattered anymore. There were other ways of attaining money, but there was only one way for John Ramshaw to bring peace to his grieving family.

chapter **TEN**

Roy lay sprawled on his back in the bed of Tom's truck, his lower legs dangling off the edge of the tailgate. Empty bottles and cans poked at his back, but he didn't pay much attention to the pain. His left arm was folded, his palm resting flat on his chest, a lit cigarette burning between his index and middle fingers. His right arm rested at his side, his hand clutching a can of beer. His tenth of the night. Or was it the eleventh? He couldn't remember and didn't care.

He felt horrible. Not from the beers he'd drank but from the way he had spoken to his wife when he called her earlier. It had felt so good at the time, so good and so justifiably right, but as soon as he'd ended the call—and in every minute that had passed since then—the guilt had weighed heavily on his mind.

With his headlamp off to conserve what juice was left in the batteries, he stared up into the night sky, amazed at the sheer number of stars that twinkled there. This deep in the woods, with no street-lamps or other lights from civilization to drown out the glow of the heavens, Roy could clearly see the spiraling arm of the Milky Way. He wondered if it had always been there. Surely it had been. Things like that didn't just suddenly appear. It had always been there, for billions of years, and he just hadn't bothered to look up and notice it before now.

Just like he'd never noticed how poorly he had treated his wife. Of course, the mistreatment had gone both ways in their marriage, but as the man in the relationship, he figured he was supposed to be the stronger of the two. The one who didn't dole out the abuse or add to the chaos in any way. He should have been the one to grin and bear it.

This realization brought a strange feeling to his heart. An odd kind of warmth. Softness where there had been none before. Roy figured that must be what growth felt like. It was funny, now that he stopped and thought about it. He seemed to do all his growing after he'd consumed about a dozen beers. But he supposed that it didn't matter how he grew. All that mattered was that he did.

He sat up slowly, squeezing his eyes closed to keep the world from spinning. He tilted his head back and downed the last of the beer he held in his hand before tossing the empty can into the bed of the truck behind him, where it landed with a clink amongst the many others. He took one last puff from his cigarette before flicking it to the ground. Then, he slid off the tailgate, stretched, and walked around the truck. He stopped just before he arrived at the cab and reached over into the bed where the cooler was nestled beneath the pickup's back glass. He withdrew two cans of cold beer from it and closed the lid of the cooler. He opened the passenger door and pulled himself up into the cab.

Once seated inside, he reached out to pull the door closed. He missed the handle and almost fell out onto the ground. Giggling, he tried again to close the door. This time, he was successful.

His intention was to start the truck and warm up a bit. He was disappointed, however, when he leaned across the bench seat, reached for the ignition, and found no keys hanging there.

"Damn it, Tom," he muttered. He straightened up, put his back against the passenger seat, and popped the top of the first of the two beers he'd fetched from the cooler. He took a long swig and let his head fall back against the head rest.

"Who the hell takes the keys with them when they're in the middle of no damn where?" he asked the empty truck.

On a whim, he stretched across the seat again and flipped down the sun visor, thinking maybe Tom had stuck the keys up there to hide them from whoever he thought might try to steal his heap of a vehicle. Nothing. He checked the ashtray but again found nothing other than loose change. He laid over on the seat, stretching out as far as he could, and plunged his hand into the darkness of the driver side floorboard. Finding nothing there, he felt around beneath the seat on the driver's side. Again, he found nothing.

"Damn it," he said, returning to the upright position. He sucked from the can, swallowing half of the contents in three deep swallows. He belched loudly, trying to think of any other place someone might hide keys. "Ah," he said, eyeing the glove box. It was the last place he could think to look. If they weren't in there, that meant they were in one of Tom's pockets somewhere out in the woods. "Here goes nothin'."

Roy worked the latch until the door of the glovebox unfastened. He moved his hand and let the thing fall open with a creak. Then he delved into it, working his way past papers and a screwdriver and a pair of pliers, searching for the keys. He didn't find them, but he did find something that piqued his interest.

Withdrawing his hand, Roy clutched the item between his thumb and forefinger. It was soft. Like silk.

He smiled. "Well well well. What do we have here, Tom, ol' buddy?" Roy set the can of beer between his legs and turned on his flashlight, aiming the weak beam at the item he held.

His grin widened as he feasted his eyes upon a small pair of underwear. His calloused fingers had been right when they deemed the fabric to be silk. They were red, the color Roy had always assigned to sex. Red lipstick. Red high heels. Red negligees. All things red were a turn-on for Roy, and these panties were as red as red could be.

Turning them around in his hands, he saw the tiny strip of fabric that constituted the back side. A thong. That made the panty even sexier. "Nice," he said, nodding his head. "Tom, you dirty dog." If the man was there, he would've offered up his fist for a bump that said *way to go, brother*. But he wasn't there. Roy was alone.

After looking out all the windows of the truck to make sure of the fact that no one else was around, Roy brought the panties to

74

his face, closed his eyes, covered his nose with the delicate fabric, and inhaled deeply, imagining a woman wearing these panties and nothing else, beckoning him to her.

As the scent entered his nose and his brain registered the aroma, he quickly withdrew the panties from his face. His eyes opened wide before narrowing with suspicion. "Wait a minute." He then sniffed them again. "You have *got* to be kiddin' me." He held the familiar-smelling panties up, stretched them out, and studied them more closely.

The tiny red bow on the center of the front.

The narrow strip of lace that lined the slim waistband.

Roy knew the panties well. After all, he had been the one to purchase them.

"Son of a bitch," he spat, throwing the panties against the windshield and watching as they dropped onto the dusty, cracked dashboard.

How could he? How could Tom, his lifelong friend, do something like this to him? How could he go behind his back and sleep with his girlfriend?

Okay, so Destiny wasn't his girlfriend now, but she had been. And Tom knew that.

He suddenly wondered if that was what Linda had been referring to on the phone. It must be. She had known about the two of them, knew that they were a...a *thing*. An item. A couple. Roy almost couldn't bring himself to think about it.

Tom and Destiny.

Together.

Kissing.

Writhing.

Yuck.

"If Linda knows," he wondered aloud, "who the hell else knows?" The whole town, most likely. And Luke. Did he know? Were he and Tom out there in the woods right now laughing at Roy for being too stupid to figure out that Tom was bedding his girlfriend?

"Son of a bitch," he shouted into the empty cab.

Roy couldn't be mad. He had no right to be. He had ended his relationship with the girl a long time ago, and therefore he had no right to be angry or upset. And yet, he was. He couldn't help himself.

He drank the rest of the beer and popped the top on the other one as memories flooded his mind. Things he and Destiny had done together. Places they'd gone. Conversations they'd had. Love they'd made. He wondered if she had told Tom she loved him the way she'd told Roy. Did she make Tom feel the way she'd made Roy feel? Did she do the things to him in bed that she'd done to Roy?

His stomach turned.

He felt betrayed. He felt stupid. How could he not see what had been going on right under his nose? How could he be so blind? He felt lied to. He felt like...like he'd been cheated on.

"Holy shit," he said, as it dawned on him that he was feeling exactly how Linda must've felt when she found out that he had cheated on her. Only she had probably felt a lot worse than he did because it was her husband that had betrayed her. A man who had sworn to love her and be honest and faithful to her until one of them died. Not some ex that she had broken up with years before that she should've never had in the first place.

He sighed, once again feeling like a heel.

"God, Linda was right," he said to the truck's empty interior. "I am an asshole. A huge, selfish, piece of shit asshole."

Then, he thought of Tom and Destiny together, wondering if she made him feel as good as she'd made Roy feel. Most likely, she did. And after all the shit Tom had been through in his life, Roy figured his friend deserved some happiness. Deserved to feel good about himself. Even if it was because of Destiny.

He finished the second beer as the urge to pee overwhelmed him. He got out of the truck and walked to the back of it, stumbling as he went. He did what was necessary to take a piss, which included unfastening a lot of zippers and buttons and sliding the front of the fanny pack around to the side, letting it hand off his hip. All tasks that were easily managed when he was sober, but not so much when he wasn't. And though the alcohol coursing through his system had dulled his senses and warmed him to the cold night air, his bare fingers fully registered the low temperatures. The joints had stiffened and struggled to perform their required duties. The whole situation was annoying and elicited from Roy more than a few cuss words, but it was nothing another beer or three wouldn't fix.

Roy swayed on his feet as the hot yellow stream poured out of him. He kept his eyes closed to better maintain his balance, a trick he had learned long ago.

Puckering his lips, Roy began to whistle. Or at least he attempted to whistle. In his inebriated state, the sound his mouth produced was little more than that of hot, yeasty wind, blown forcefully through awkwardly pursed lips. But in his mind, it sounded just like his favorite song. A country tune about a man whose wife left him and took the dog and truck with her.

Behind him, a twig snapped.

Roy stopped whistling mid-tune. He tried to stop pissing but couldn't end the stream. He turned his head, looking over his shoulder and listening intently for any other sounds, but all he heard was the sound of his urine falling on dead leaves.

It only took Roy a couple of seconds to forget about the sound he'd heard. It wasn't that he'd convinced himself he hadn't heard it or that he felt it was nothing to worry about. It was that in his foggy state, his mind wandered on to other things before he had a chance to process the danger he might be in or the fear he should feel.

As he zipped his pants, he belched loudly and farted.

"That sounded like shit," he said to himself. It was a lame joke, and one that had grown old with overuse, but it struck him as hilarious and sent him into a fit of laughter. As he turned around, he threw his head back and cackled into the night sky, his breath escaping him as a series of little clouds. This move threw off his balance and caused him to stumble and fall. He tried to remain on his feet, which only made matters worse. He gave up and went down, falling on his left side before rolling onto his back. He laughed until the joke no longer seemed funny. Then, he fell silent, staring up into the darkness of the universe and the billions of stars that lay within.

As his eyelids grew heavy and each blink lasted longer than the one before it, Roy felt himself slipping away into a dream world where no hungry bigfoots or angry wives waited for him.

chapter **ELEVEN**

Once Tom's gagging fit passed, Luke asked, "Are you going to be okay?" He studied his friend, hoping he would say yes and mean it.

"Yeah. I'll be fine," Tom wheezed.

Watching the large man struggle to breathe, Luke knew that he wouldn't be fine. Climbing the steep hill had damn near done him in. He had wheezed his way into a coughing fit, which led to a series of gags, that eventually turned into several minutes of vomiting. He was now sitting on a fallen tree, elbows on his knees, spit falling in long strands down to the puddle of puke that lay between his feet.

Luke could stay silent on the matter no longer. "Tom, I think you need to see a doctor."

"Why? I know what they look like."

Ignoring the joke, Luke said, "What do you mean why? Look at you. You've been struggling all night. And this...well this is just crazy, what you're doing now."

"What are you talkin' about? What am I doin'?" He retched again.

"Look at you! You can't breathe and you're puking."

"So?"

"So I can't carry you out of here if you drop dead. And it looks like that's what you're going to end up doing. Didn't you tell me your dad had a heart attack? Don't you think this is something you should be keeping an eye on?"

"Dad has a flutter. And I'll be fine," he waved his hand at Luke, dismissing his worries.

Luke rolled his eyes and threw up his arms. "Oh sure. You'll be fine. You've been saying that all night, and yet you've been steadily getting worse."

"So I have a little trouble breathin' when I exert myself," Tom said as if it was normal for him to gasp for air like a fish on land. "Big deal."

"It is a big deal. You don't just struggle when you exert yourself, Tom. You struggle to breathe when you're walking on flat ground. You struggle harder when you walk up—or *down*—hills. You struggle to breathe when you laugh, for god's sake. That's not normal. And throwing up from walking…nobody does that. I didn't do that, and I just walked up the same hill you did."

Tom looked at Luke and said, "Yeah, but that was a steep ass hill."

Luke looked over his shoulder and down the hill they had just climbed, which would more accurately be described as a mountain. Looking back at Tom, he said, "Yeah, okay. That was a steep one, but still. I'm not crumpled up on a tree puking on my shoes and gasping for air the way you are."

Tom remained silent for a moment, spitting every few seconds. Then he asked, "So what do you want me to do, Whistlepig?"

"I'd like you to see a doctor. A real doctor. A heart doctor."

Tom considered this and said, "Fine. If it'll shut you up, I'll see a doctor." He wasn't surprised at his friend's request. In all honesty, he had been toying with the idea of seeing a heart specialist for the past few months. He knew something wasn't right in his body. And with his dad having all his troubles, he was afraid he was dooming himself to follow in the old man's shoes if he didn't do something soon.

"Really?"

"Really. Now shut the hell up and help me get up off this tree."

"No."

Tom looked at Luke, shocked at his refusal to help. He waited for an explanation.

He didn't have to wait long.

"I'm not helping you up. I don't think you should go any farther. I think I should go by myself while you stay here and rest. When I come back, we'll walk—slowly—to the truck. I don't need you having a damn heart attack out here and dying on me. There have been more than enough deaths today. We don't need another one."

"Damn it, Luke. I said I'm fine."

"I could say I'm rich, but that doesn't mean I am."

"Yeah, but I *am* fine."

"Tom, so help me, if you tell me you're fine one more time, I'll cut a switch and whip you with it."

"I'm tempted to say it again just to watch you try to whip me."

"Don't think I won't do it."

"Oh, I'm sure you'd try. But I'd squash you like a bug."

Luke shook his head and grinned. "I'll tell you what. You stay here and let me go do this by myself, and I'll let you squash me like a bug later."

"Alright. Fine. Go," he said with a wave of his hand. "Kill the thing by your damn self then. Glory hog. That's what I'm gonna start callin' you. No more Whistlepig. You're Glory Hog now."

"Hey, I don't want to go by myself. You think I want to face that thing alone? Hell no. I'm just trying to save your stupid ass and keep you from dying."

"Yeah, yeah. Save it for your press conference. And hey, maybe they'll put that on your medal."

"I'm going now. You stay right there. Don't move from that spot. I mean it. I don't really know where the hell I am, so if I manage to find my way back to you and you're not here, I'm not looking for you. I'm heading straight back to the truck. Assuming I can find it."

"You won't have any trouble finding your way back, ya damn bloodhound."

He was right, of course. But Luke wasn't worried about making it back as much as he was about going forward. He was in unfamiliar territory. Though the whole county was pretty much the same, with one section of the forest looking just like all the rest, the fact was he'd never stepped foot in this part of the woods. He didn't know the lay of the land. Didn't know if there were sinkholes or caves or where the private property lines were. But those weren't the things that really concerned Luke. What was really bothering him was the uncertainty of whether or not Tom would still be alive when he got back.

Well, that and facing the man-killer alone.

"Just stay put all the same. Rest up. We'll head back together in a bit. I'm going that way," he said, pointing in the direction to their right. "I won't go too far because I feel that we probably should get you back to town pretty soon. But you can't go back until you've rested, so while you're doing that, I'm going to search a little farther. I'll be back soon."

"I'll wait here then."

Luke turned and walked away, heading along the ridge line and away from Tom. He didn't make it more than a few steps before Tom spoke.

He said, "Hey, Luke?"

Luke turned to hear what his friend had to say. In a serious tone, Tom said, "Come back to me. I love you." He then busted out laughing, which quickly turned to coughing.

"Real funny. Is this how you want to die? Making stupid jokes and puking on your shoes? Knock it off. Take slow, deep breaths. Try to stay alive until I get back." He turned and walked away once more, not looking back this time no matter how much Tom's coughing worried him.

chapter **TWELVE**

Roy pushed himself up from the cold ground and stumbled toward the truck. He managed to pull himself up into the cluttered bed and onto the roof of the cab. "Damn woman," he muttered, pulling his cell phone out of his pocket. He fumbled with the thing until he managed to dial his home number. As he listened to the phone ring at his house, he swayed and said, "Pick up the phone, Linda. Damn."

When his wife finally answered, instead of hello, she said, "This better not be you, Roy."

"It's me, baby. Listen, I'm sorry."

"About what?"

"What do you mean about what? About before." He swayed again.

"I thought maybe you had come to your senses and called to say you were sorry about the other stuff." The sleepiness left her voice as she spoke.

"What other stuff?"

"You know."

"Baby, if I knew, I wouldn't be askin'."

"About the lies, Roy. All the dirty lies. About leaving me here alone—"

"Oh, here we go."

"—while you were out gallivanting with some whore."

"Gallivantin'? Who the hell gallivants? I wasn't gallivantin', Linda. And she's not a whore." At least he hadn't thought of her like that back when he was sneaking around seeing her. But he certainly thought of her that way now.

"Still taking up for her, I see."

Roy imagined her pushing herself up in bed and crossing her arms over her ample chest, bracing for the fight she'd been longing to have for so long.

"Damn it, Linda, I'm not takin' up for her. I'm just sayin' that she's not a whore. That's all. I wouldn't cheat on you with a whore."

"Oh, so you *would* cheat on me with someone who wasn't a whore?"

Roy tilted his head back and rolled his eyes, a move which made him stagger on the roof of the truck. He hadn't called home looking for a fight. He'd called to tell his wife how sorry he was for making her feel the way he currently felt. He had thought that perhaps the two of them could commiserate in their heartache. Instead, his wife was pouncing on the opportunity to twist the knife in his chest. "I wouldn't cheat on you with a whore, not a whore, it doesn't matter. I wouldn't cheat on you, Linda. Period."

"Except you did."

Roy sighed.

"With a whore."

"Oh my god, Linda. Damn. I call to say I'm sorry, and this is what I get? Why can't you just let it go?"

"Why can't you just keep it in your pants?"

Roy pulled the phone away from his ear and yelled into the night. It was a guttural yell, one that released a whole lot of pent-up frustration that he had been keeping pushed way down inside for a long time. It felt good to release it.

With the phone to his ear once again, he said, "Linda, I'm sorry I cheated on you. I've told you a million times that it won't happen again."

"Yes, but you told me a million times that it would never happen in the first place. And then it did. So how can I believe you?"

"Because I'm tellin' you. I won't."

"But you also told me you wouldn't, and then you did."

"Damn it, Linda, why are you like this?" he asked, swaying back and forth. This time, he had to hold one arm out to maintain his balance.

"Why are you a cheater?"

"I don't know, Linda. Why are you a bitch?" Roy knew he had messed up when he heard the click come from the other end of the call. "Linda?" He pulled the phone away from his ear and looked at the screen, fearing he had lost the signal. He moved the phone around, up and over, back and forth, keeping his eyes on the screen, trying to attain a better signal so he could call her back. On some level, he knew the signal wasn't the problem. He was the problem. But he tried anyway, stepping side to side with the phone held high and then low. "Come on," he grumbled. And then he saw it. A fourth bar. A strong signal. He smiled, thinking of what he would say to Linda when he called her back. But before he had a chance to dial the first in the series of numbers, he misplaced his left foot, his boot missing the truck's roof and finding nothing but air.

The distance from the roof of the truck to the ground was maybe seven feet, but it felt like a lot more as he was falling. It took Roy half of the fall to realize he was falling and the other half to say, "Oh, shit."

The abrupt stop at the end of the fall knocked the wind out of him. When he caught his breath, he grunted and groaned and moaned and rolled onto his side. He tested various body parts and noted that all seemed to be functioning properly, which was good. Although, when Linda got through with him, he might not be able to say the same thing.

He thought about their phone call, not bothering to get up from the ground. What was the point of getting up anyway? He could get up and be miserable or he could stay where he was and feel just as shitty. It took less effort to stay put.

Why did Linda always have to be that way? Why did every argument always have to circle back to the one damn time he had failed her, the one time he had been weak and had cheated on her? It was over and done with, in the past. Why couldn't she just move on?

Because, Roy realized, it wasn't just one time. Sure, it was one affair with one person. But there had been many, many instances of Roy being unfaithful to his wife with that one person, of him lying to his wife and sneaking around behind her back. Maybe that's what the root of the problem really was. For both Roy and Linda. He hadn't simply cheated one time. Every time he'd kissed Destiny, every time he'd held her hand or made love to her or spent time with her or even thought about her, it was another time he'd cheated on his wife. And when you thought of it that way and did the math on the matter, that was a hell of a lot of cheating he'd done.

As he pondered the subject, he imagined what it would be like if their roles were reversed. If she had been the one to cheat on him, would he be so eager to forgive and forget? He didn't think so, especially given the way he felt now, knowing that his friend was sleeping with his ex-girlfriend. Roy was an easy-going guy, but even he had his limits.

"Ah, shit," he muttered, knowing that he was going to apologize and make it up to his wife if it was the last thing he ever did. But it wasn't going to happen tonight. He could call her a hundred more times, and she would most likely not answer a single one of those calls. Besides, if he climbed up on that roof to make a call once more and fell off again, he might not be lucky enough to escape with all his parts in working order. It was better to stay safe than to be sorry.

"Nothin' safer than the ground," he said with a smile, patting the earth beside him.

It was then that he felt something wet drip onto the side of his face. Rain, he thought. No. Not rain. Something else. Something…warm. Bird piss, perhaps. Roy wiped the wetness away, bringing his fingers to his nose and inhaling. It smelled of rancid meat. What the hell could possibly smell like that out here, he wondered?

Then, suddenly, he knew.

85

chapter **THIRTEEN**

Luke promised Tom he wouldn't go far, but that was before he stepped in a pile of animal scat. Though it wasn't still steaming, it was fresh. He could tell by the squish of it beneath his foot and the smell of it, ripe and pungent. After wiping what he could off the bottom of his shoe with a stick and a clump of dead leaves, he decided to continue the search, knowing he must be close to finding the damn thing.

He wondered if it slept. Was it possible that he could simply walk up on it while it was napping?

Possible, yes. Probable, no. If Luke was a man born with that kind of luck, he would've played the lottery a lot more than he did.

Luke walked lightly, listening to the sounds of the night around him. Somewhere nearby, an owl hooted. In the far distance, a pack of coyotes yipped. It seemed like such an ordinary night, which was odd considering the amount of carnage that had taken place in these very woods and the mission that Luke was now on.

It was such a strange feeling to simultaneously want to find the thing and yet not find it at all. If there was a metaphor for life in there, he didn't see it. Probably couldn't see the forest for the trees, whatever the hell that meant.

Metaphors were stupid.

In his pocket, his phone rang, startling him. The sound seemed out of place so deep in the forest. For a second, he was too stunned to move. He hadn't heard the sound in hours, and he certainly hadn't expected to hear it now. But it was ringing all the same.

When he finally forced himself into action, he pulled it from his pocket, saw Susan's name on the glowing screen, and touched it before pressing the device to his ear with a smile on his face.

"Hello?" he said, excited to hear his wife's voice.

But there was only silence.

"Hello? Susan?"

Static. He checked the screen and saw that they were still connected. He put the phone against his ear again and said, "Susan, can you hear me?"

She didn't reply. He knew from previous experiences that it was possible for her to hear him even though he couldn't hear her. If that was the case, she might be listening right now.

"Susan, listen. If you can hear me, we're still in the woods. We're hunting for the animal that killed Paul's Ramshaw's little girl this morning. Well, I guess technically it was yesterday morning. We found another guy out in the woods that was attacked. Roy went to call for help. We have no service out here, so I can't call you. I'm surprised you got through to me. I'll be home as soon as I can. I love—"

The call ended. It was dropped before he could tell her he loved her.

"Damn it," he said, looking angrily at the phone as his wife's name disappeared from the screen. He returned the thing to his pocket, hoping she at least heard some of what he had said. And as far as her not hearing him say he loved her, that wasn't a big deal because she knew. But still, he would've liked to have been able to say it, just in case it would turn out to be the last time he had a chance to tell her.

He was frustrated and cold and tired, and he was more than ready to head back to where Tom was waiting for him. When he turned, his light caught something off to his right. It was a heavily overgrown road. A path, really. Perhaps it had once been a road used by logging trucks, or maybe it had been a dirt road used by people who lived somewhere out here way back when, but now it was barely noticeable.

Luke looked over his shoulder, thinking about the way he had come. It wouldn't make a lot of sense to go back the exact same way. He knew that if he followed the trail, at least for a little bit, and then turned right and walked through the woods, he would end up back where he'd left Tom.

And so off he went.

To fill the silence and fight back against the creepy feeling he had of being watched, Luke sang quietly to himself as he walked. Hillbilly Highway. His favorite song. He couldn't carry a tune if it came in a bucket, but he knew all the words and sang with his heart. It did little to make him feel better.

It wasn't long until he heard something crashing through woods, something big, and it was headed his way. He stopped, gripped the rifle tighter, and waited. He prayed it wasn't the creature he was looking for, but he also hoped it was. Not for the reward. He was past that. And not for the glory, no matter what Tom thought. He just wanted the nightmare to end. He wanted everyone—the little girl's family, the mauled man's family, the entire damn county—to be able to sleep at night without worrying that there was a vicious animal roaming the woods looking to satisfy its bloodlust.

He scanned the woods, turning and listening.

Watching.

Waiting.

And sure enough, it came.

It burst from the trees on the left side of the old road, cleared the path altogether in one graceful leap, and disappeared into the thick forest on the other side of the road, coming within a couple feet of Luke.

The deer was magnificent. A big buck, ten points at least, though it all happened so fast Luke didn't have time to count them.

He breathed a sigh of relief, though he didn't fully relax. He hadn't been truly calm since he'd stepped off his porch earlier in the evening. It was mating season for deer, so the buck was probably chasing a doe. But Luke hadn't seen a doe. If it wasn't chasing something, that meant it was running away from something.

Something large.

chapter **FOURTEEN**

Roy quickly rolled under the truck, his heart pounding in his ears. He thought maybe he was wrong. Maybe he had what Linda often referred to as beer brain, where what he saw and heard was half real, half imagined.

He slowly scooted forward, peering out from under the truck, trying to get a better look and be sure.

The animal saw him, threw its head back, and roared, spit hanging from its open maw in long strands.

Yup. That's what he thought.

Roy quickly pushed himself back under the truck, staying as close to the center as he could.

A minute passed.

Then another.

With him lying flat on the ground, the cold soon began to penetrate the layers of clothing and seep into his bones, despite the warmth of the beer that coursed through his body. He hoped he didn't have to stay there very long.

Linda was right. He shouldn't have given Luke his gun.

It was too dark for Roy to see the thing's feet, to know whether or not the thing was still standing there, so he turned on his headlamp and aimed it in the direction of where the monster had been when it roared at him.

No feet.

He turned his head, the light following to the left and then the right.

Still no feet.

Where the hell did it go, he wondered. And how was it so quiet? The damn thing was massive. It should've made all kinds of noise walking through the woods. It should've crunched leaves. It should've snapped twigs. Hell, the whole earth should've shaken under its weight. Yet it hadn't made a sound. It had crept up on him in silence. Terrifying silence, which was all that Roy heard now.

He waited for a while, giving the creature enough time to get far away from him and the truck. And then he waited longer. He waited until his teeth began to chatter and his toes went numb in his boots.

Then he waited a little longer.

The beam of his flashlight dwindled away as the batteries slowly died.

Then, reluctantly, he slowly and quietly scooted to the edge of the truck. He poked his head out and peered around with the dying light but found nothing. Assuming the thing had given up and gone on to find easier prey, he crawled out from under the vehicle and stood up, his heart thudding in his chest.

There was no other sound aside from any that he made himself. Of course, that didn't mean a damn thing seeing as there was no sound before the thing seemingly materialized out of thin air, but Roy pushed that out of his mind and thought about what he was going to do next.

Call the police.

But he had already done that. They should arrive any minute, assuming they could find him based off the shitty directions he had given them.

Call Linda.

But why? He had already called her twice, and each time the call had ended badly. She couldn't help him now, and that was assuming she even answered the phone when he called.

Yell for Luke and Tom.

Except that wasn't a good idea. They were probably too far away to hear his shouts, and even if they were nearby and could hear him, yelling would only attract the beast if it was still close by. And Roy felt that it was. Even though he couldn't see or hear it, he knew it was somewhere nearby watching him. Hungry for him. Looking for the perfect opportunity to sink its sharp teeth into Roy's flesh.

That feeling of being watched, of not being alone, was unsettling to Roy. It unnerved him in the deepest way. He could only think of one thing to do to ease that feeling and calm his nerves.

"Put a beer on it," he whispered for no other reason than to hear a voice.

Looking around once more to make sure the thing was gone, Roy moved, wobbling on unsteady legs. He reached over the side of the bed of the truck, popping open the lid of the cooler and plunging his hand into the depths of it. He knew there were more beers inside, as he'd made sure to pack plenty before leaving home. But he couldn't find any now.

The cooler was large and stretched almost entirely across the width of the truck. In height, it towered a couple of inches over the side of the bed, which meant Roy couldn't reach the bottom of it. And he certainly couldn't reach all the way across to the other side of it. Not from where he stood.

He stepped forward, pressing his chest against the cold metal of the truck bed. His fingertips grazed the bottom of the plastic container, yet he still didn't find a beer.

"Damn it," he muttered.

He stretched his body as far as he could, standing on the tips of his toes. His fingers searched the cooler, back and forth, further and further until at last they made contact with the object of Roy's desire. He grabbed it, pulled it toward him, and smiled. It had been a long, rough day, an even longer and rougher night, and this was just what he needed to make it all better. His mouth filled with saliva at the thought of it.

Suddenly, a set of long, sharp claws ripped through the layers of clothing he wore and tore through the flesh of Roy's back as if both were made of tissue paper.

Roy screamed as every muscle in his body tensed. His hands clenched, crushing the can and sending the frothy liquid inside running down his arm, soaking the sleeve of his coat, just as his blood soaked the back of it.

The animal roared and struck again, slicing through the thin skin that stretched across Roy's ribs. He cried out in pain, dropping the crushed and now empty can into the bed of the truck. Without taking the time to think or wonder or strategize, he moved, running left, toward the back of the truck and hopefully out of reach of the beast.

Another roar. The sound was so close, it hurt his ears and vibrated his chest.

Roy made a right turn at the tail light and headed around the truck, passing the open tailgate. He forgot he had left it down, slammed into it, and knocked himself off balance. He stumbled, almost fell, but managed to remain upright.

He heard the shuffle of feet sliding across leaves and rocks, wondered briefly whether it was his own footsteps or those of the monster behind him, and then he moved around to the other side of the vehicle.

He suddenly felt as if having his back turned toward the animal was the stupidest thing he could do in that moment, so he whirled around, shining the dimming light on whatever may be creeping up behind him, ready to strike once more.

There was nothing there. The thing wasn't sneaking up behind him.

Roy felt the warm blood—*his* warm blood—running down his back and side and soaking his underwear. He knew it was bad. He clutched his ribs with his left hand, intending to apply pressure to the wound. But instead, his fingers slipped inside his body, sliding with ease between his exposed ribs and shredded skin.

There were so many things Roy didn't know. He didn't know what women wanted. He didn't know how to do his income taxes. He didn't know what kept planes in the air. But he knew for damn sure that any time he could put his hand inside his own body, it meant that he was screwed.

And Roy Johnston was screwed.

chapter **FIFTEEN**

Tree limbs slapped against Luke's face, scratching his cheeks and forehead and leaving welts and abrasions in their wake. He carried the rifle in his left arm and used his right to ward off as many of the low-hanging branches as he could. But he couldn't stop them all.

He made his way through the woods, following the smell of smoke which came to him carried on the wind, the faint scent of burning pine tickling his sensitive nose. The smell was familiar, one that Luke knew well.

Had it not been deer season, the scent of burning wood would've been oddly placed so deep in the forest on such a cold night, but as it were, the odor gave no cause for alarm. It simply meant that there was a campfire nearby, most likely belonging to a group of deer hunters. Now, nearly half an hour after first detecting the smell in the air, the odor was much stronger than before, proof that Luke was moving in the right direction and getting closer to the source.

The aroma stirred memories for Luke. Memories of camping with his family as a kid, and then of camping with his own family as an adult. It also brought to mind all the times he and his friends had gathered together on the banks of the river on the weekends to build a bonfire and then stand around it sharing stories and laughs while drinking beer and enjoying their youth. Some of his best memories lay on the rocky shores of the river. And nearly all of them were accompanied by the odor of burning wood.

Gradually, his thoughts turned from days gone by to the present. To Roy, who was hopefully leading the police to the unfortunate man's remains. And to Tom, who sat on that fallen tree, waiting for Luke to return. He had promised his friend he wouldn't be gone long, but it had already been over an hour since he'd made that vow. Yet instead of going back to where he'd left Tom, sick and miserable, he traveled farther and farther away from him, which meant that it would take him even longer to get back. An hour out meant an hour back. Tom was bound to worry, but Luke couldn't help it. He needed to warn the campers of the danger they were in and do his best to convince them to get the hell out of the woods while they still could.

If he wasn't already too late.

He pushed that thought aside and trekked on, following his nose toward the source of the smell.

Finally, several minutes later, Luke saw an orange glow up ahead. He couldn't see the flames yet, but he didn't need to see them to know he had found the campfire. The sight of it gave him a burst of energy and propelled him forward faster now, erasing the feeling that the search would go on forever only to prove futile in the end.

Luke dashed through the forest, keeping his eyes on the destination ahead while carefully navigating through and around the thick underbrush, the low-hanging tree limbs, and the giant trees that had been blown down during storms with high winds.

He wanted to shout and yell and scream his warnings to the campers, but he fought the urge to do so, knowing that the sound of his shouts might alert the creature to his presence, should it be in the immediate vicinity.

A thought occurred to Luke then, as his legs continued to carry him toward the fire's glow. If the campers were deer hunters—and Luke was almost positive they were—that meant they were armed. Nearly everyone in the south owned at least one gun. Not everybody kept their weapons loaded while they were at home, but

94

nearly everyone kept them loaded at camp. Especially while hunting. So unless Luke was looking to get shot, he couldn't just run into a stranger's camp in the middle of the night while carrying a gun and expect them to welcome him with open arms. Southern hospitality could only be extended so far. He needed to announce his arrival.

Therein laid the conundrum. It was a risky move to call out to the campers, but it was an even riskier move to remain silent. Calling out *might* get him mauled by a wild animal, but not calling out would almost certainly get him shot.

"Hey," Luke shouted as he drew closer to the camp. He could clearly see the campfire now, the bright orange and yellow flames reaching toward the sky like thin, dancing arms.

He slowed his pace to a walk now, stepping around the pile of chopped wood that had been haphazardly stacked by the campers earlier in the day. Possibly even days before. There was no way to tell how long the hunters had been there, but the camp site itself was a pretty good indicator that they'd been settled in for a quite some time.

The camper was old. Most likely an early 1970s model. It didn't help the aging process any that the thing hadn't been very well taken care of. One window had duct tape covering a crack that ran both the height and the width of it, while another window was missing altogether. A piece of plywood, gray from age and weather, had taken the place of the pane of glass that should've been in the aluminum frame. The door was an old house door that had been cut down to size in order to fit the opening. The metal siding was mostly rust. The camper had seen better days, for sure.

To the right of the door was an old folding table, which was almost as rusty as the camper it accompanied. Two of the legs were bent, so one end of it set lower than the other, meaning nothing that rolled could be placed on the table's top. The uneven surface was littered with chaotically strewn pots, bowls with grime caked on them, a small scale for weighing food, and various other items that Luke didn't bother trying to identify in the dark.

On the other side of the camp fire, opposite from where Luke stopped to catch his breath and take in his surroundings, there was a truck with the driver's door open parked beside an ATV.

The place wasn't much in the way of deer camps.

"Hey," Luke shouted again. "Can anyone hear me? I need to talk to you. It's urgent."

He expected to see the rickety door of the camper thrown open by a sleepy hunter, grumbling as he stepped out into the cold to see what all the yelling was about. But the door remained closed, and the camp remained silent except for the crackling of the fire.

Luke walked toward the camper, scrunching his face as the smell hit his nose. It was the pungent odor of ammonia. Piss. More specifically, cat piss. The closer he got to the old camper, the stronger the smell became. His eyes watered. His throat burned. Luke coughed. Then he gagged. He stopped, doubled over, and fought the urge to vomit. When it passed, he stood and moved again, vowing to get this over with so he could get away from that stench.

Breathing only through his mouth, he knocked on the door, yelling while he did it to lessen the chance of him being mistaken for a thief or a murderer. The last thing he wanted to do was avoid being killed by an animal only to be killed by a hunter.

After a minute passed without the door opening or any sounds coming from inside the camper that would lead him to believe someone was awake and moving around, he knocked again. Louder this time. Still, no answer came. Could be a heavy sleeper in there, Luke thought, knowing damn well that wasn't the case.

Hoping to have better luck if he showed urgency and a smidgeon of hostility, he pounded on the door.

"Hey," he said in the gruffest voice he could muster. "Open up. There's an emergency out here."

Luke accidentally inhaled through his nose, drawing a lungful of the powerful smell into his nostrils and down his esophagus. He gagged, wondering why the hell there was enough cat urine out there to gag a grown man.

Perhaps it wasn't that it was an abundance of urine, he thought. Maybe it was just his sensitive nose making it seem like a lot of piss.

Or maybe it really was a lot of piss. There were bobcats and mountain lions that roamed all over the county. While bobcats weren't big enough to produce an abnormal amount of pee in one go, a cougar certainly was. Those things weighed as much as an adult human, so Luke imagined their bladders could probably hold a lot of the stinky liquid.

But still, would it be enough to give off an aroma this strong? He doubted it.

Luke knocked again and waited.

No response.

He banged on the door, knowing it would produce nothing more than the other bangs had. When the silence proved him right, Luke turned around, taking in the scene more closely. This time, he noticed that the items on the table next to the older camper were more than just messily strewn. They had been knocked around, some overturning on the table, others falling to the ground. And the table itself had been moved. It stood with one end touching the side of the camper and the opposite end a few feet away, at an awkward angle.

He looked at the camper, shone his light across the side of it, and saw a dent large enough to accommodate a man.

Aiming his light at the ground, Luke noticed long sections of dirt that had been disturbed. Places where a person might have tried to dig in their feet for better traction. Places where a struggle had taken place.

Luke's insides twisted as he realized that his worst fear may be his reality. He might be too late to save this person. Or even worse, these people.

He quickly went to the truck, a red Chevy, and stepped around the open door. He stood in the doorway, his eyes scanning all that was illuminated in the beam of his flashlight. Without thinking, Luke gasped and took a step back, not wanting to believe that the grisly tableau was real.

What was left of the driver was spilled across the seat. It didn't amount to much more than part of one arm and most of his torso and head, sans one eyeball. On the ground, steam still rose from the puddle of the man's blood that had settled there. Bits of flesh and bone were scattered throughout the mess, leaving no doubt as to what had happened there.

"Oh my god," Luke muttered. There was a tingle at the base of his neck that caused the tiny hairs there to stand erect. The tingle either brought with it or was the result of the sense of not being alone. The unsettling feeling that someone or something was nearby, watching him.

Luke spun around, making sure the damn thing wasn't sneaking up on him. Seeing nothing, he pulled his cell phone from his pocket and checked to see if he had a signal strong enough to call home and tell Susan he loved her one more time. Just in case. But the device registered no signal at all. "Damn it," he said, turning the worthless thing off. Then he remembered something his daughter had taught him. He could schedule a text. That way, if he did get mauled to death and was unable to tell his family how he felt, his phone would tell them for him later.

Quickly, Luke typed out his message:

> Love u Susan
> Love u Hope
> I tried my best

He scheduled it to send at noon the following day. Whatever was going to happen would be over by then. Whether he walked in the front door of his house or the coroner scooped him off the forest floor and took him back to town in a body bag, it would happen before noon.

Before Luke returned the phone to his pocket, he remembered a movie Susan had made him watch one time in which a man died but his wife continued receiving letters from him for years after his death. Susan had loved it, but Luke had rolled his eyes at the premise. It was cheesy and over-the-top romantic, something that would never happen in real life. But now that he was in a situation where he could die and leave his wife and daughter behind to mourn his absence, it didn't seem so stupid. In fact, it was downright brilliant.

He typed out several more text messages, scheduling each one further and further into the future, smiling at the thought of Susan and Hope finding comfort in them one day. If he was lucky, he'd be there to see their faces when they received them. Then he could tease them for getting all misty-eyed over him.

Finally, he returned the phone to his pocket and sighed. Sending the texts had made him feel good, but it also made him feel like shit. What the hell was he doing? Why was he out here, traipsing through the woods in search of a creature that he clearly wasn't equipped to deal with? This wasn't a job for a guy who had worked all day and skipped supper. A guy who was in no way an avid hunter. A guy whose total knowledge of animals could fit on the head of a dime with plenty of room to spare. He didn't belong out here. This was a job for someone with a little more courage and a lot less common sense than Luke possessed, because that's what it was going to take to bring an end to this nightmare.

Luke stood by the fire, warming himself while looking around the camp. He figured he should look for the others, but he didn't know why. If there was someone left alive, someone the beast hadn't ripped to shreds and feasted on, they would have come out and made themselves known by now. He could think of no other reason to search the camp and its surroundings for the remains of the rest of the campers. He couldn't stand the thought of finding another person the way he'd found the last two. The mere thought of it made his stomach twist and turn.

Luke Davis was built for many things but finding bits and pieces of people wasn't one of them.

chapter **SIXTEEN**

Tom checked his watch. Luke had been gone a long time. A lot longer than he said he would be, and a hell of a lot longer than he should've been. Still, Tom had little choice but to keep waiting for him to return.

He thought about what Luke said to him about seeing a doctor. It was something he knew he needed to do, and he had already decided to make an appointment before Luke demanded he agree to go to the doctor. But he still planned to tell people that he only went to appease his friend. That way, he wouldn't look so weak. Although, now that he thought about it, he realized it wouldn't matter much how weak he looked to other people if they were looking at him lying in an open casket.

I should've eaten better, he thought. And eaten less.

Of course, his diet wasn't the only thing that led him to where he was now. Bad hearts ran in his family alongside flat feet, a broad middle, and the love of gambling. But all those tacos, cheeseburgers, pizzas, and beers couldn't have done him any favors.

Luke hadn't told Tom what to do if he didn't return, so he wasn't sure whether he should stick around and wait longer or head back to the truck. He didn't want to leave his friend alone out there in the woods, but with every minute that passed, he became more and more creeped out for a variety of reasons.

He was alone.

The woods were dark.

There was a crazy monster on the loose.

There was a dead guy out there somewhere. Or pieces of him, anyway.

And his chest was killing him. He wasn't ready to admit that he either had, was having, or was about to have a heart attack, but deep down he knew it.

Nobody ever wanted to have a heart attack, but if you were going to have one, you damn sure didn't want to be out in the middle of nowhere when it happened. Which was exactly where Tom was now.

He had told Luke he knew where they were, but that wasn't entirely true. He knew approximately where they were. The general vicinity. He had hunted in woods all over the county, but he'd never been in this particular area before. He felt almost certain that he could make his way back to the truck and to town, but when one tree looked like the next and he was in so much pain, it wouldn't be an easy chore.

Tom took comfort in the fact that if Roy had made the phone call as planned, the place was sure to be crawling with cops by now. If not now, it would be soon. He could pass the search for Luke—as well as the search for the animal—off to an officer who didn't have a family history of flat feet and bad hearts or a propensity to eat until he felt sick. The cops could do the physical work while Tom went back to the truck to wait on Luke.

He checked his watch again. It was half past three.

"Five more minutes," he said, looking around for any sign of Luke but finding none.

As the minutes passed, Tom's worry began to manifest itself physically in the winding of his intestines, the cramping of his stomach, and the tightening of his chest. What if Luke didn't come back? What if he got lost and was doomed to roam the woods until he died of exposure? What would Tom tell Susan and Hope? Or worse, what if Luke had found the animal—or the damn thing had found him—and Luke had lost the battle? Tom hadn't heard any gunshots, but if Luke was attacked from behind, he might not have had a chance to fire off a shot.

His mind raced with the many possibilities of all that could be keeping his friend from returning, none of which were good. And each new horrific idea that popped into his head, complete with graphic imagery, seemed to make his chest grow tighter and tighter until he found it nearly impossible to breathe.

Tom pressed his right hand over his chest, specifically the area over his heart. It wasn't until he brought his left arm up to check his watch again, to see if five minutes had passed yet, that he realized just how much his left arm hurt.

"Oh, shit. Not now," he said through clenched teeth as he fell forward and collapsed onto the ground.

chapter **SEVENTEEN**

Roy decided he would feel much safer if he waited for the cavalry inside the cab of the truck. The vehicle's steel frame and metal exterior were by no means impenetrable, especially to an oversized and extremely determined beast, but it beat the hell out of nothing at all. Standing outside left him feeling vulnerable and exposed. Which is exactly what he was.

Holding onto the side of the truck with his right hand to maintain his balance, Roy had to let go of his tattered ribs and use the hand that was soaked in his own blood to open the door. Covered with the slick goo, his hand slid off the handle, unable to make purchase. He groaned and tried again, hooking his bony fingers onto the handle and clutching it tightly so as not to lose his grasp again. He was shocked to discover how difficult such a simple task was for him to complete.

It was frightening to Roy to discover just how weak he had become in such a short amount of time. Perhaps it was the beer. Or maybe it was the pain. But most likely, it was the blood loss that was responsible for zapping his strength. And just like the blood spilling from his body, what strength he had left was draining fast.

Roy stumbled as he stepped back and pulled the door open. A groan escaped him. The pain really began to set in on him then. His back. His ribs. His ripped flesh. The cold air was like sharp knives stabbing into his wounds. He hurt in a way he never had before. It was a pain that no amount of beers could erase. Not that he didn't want to put a few on it and make sure.

He began to climb into the cab, putting his right leg on the floorboard and grabbing the steering wheel to pull himself up. He returned his left hand to his injured side, where he kept it tucked under his right arm, pressed tightly against his ribs, careful to keep his hand on the outside of his body this time. As his other foot left the ground, the door slammed hard against him, pinning his leg between it and the rocker panel. He howled in pain, trying to pull his leg free with no success. It was obvious the door hadn't simply closed on its own. Something was applying a great deal of pressure on the damn thing, pressure that cut straight into Roy's thin calf.

Turning his head, he looked over his shoulder and through the door's window, where he saw the monster glaring back at him. It had angry eyes, teeth as long as Roy's fingers, and was covered in dark hair which was matted with blood. The bottoms of its feet were pressed flat against the glass. At the end of those feet were claws as long the blade of a steak knife.

Roy turned his body and used both hands to push against the door, but it was no use. He wasn't strong enough to open it now, not with the massive creature pressing on it from the other side. He had barely been strong enough to open it when there wasn't a giant force working against him. Now, in the state he was currently in, he didn't stand a chance.

Hoping to have better luck with his lower appendages, Roy brought his right foot up, placed it on the door panel, and shoved, trying to push the door open far enough to free his other leg. It was a move that did nothing other than anger the creature further and send fresh waves of pain radiating throughout Roy's ribs and back.

The beast opened its mouth, spit hanging in long strands. It roared, leaving a cloud of breath on the cold glass. It then began to bounce against the door, pushing with its paws in short, rapid bursts.

Unable to stifle it, Roy released a scream that would've shattered the thickest of wine glasses. He couldn't stop the sound from escaping him. It was hard to keep the yelps to himself when there was an animal that weighed hundreds of pounds putting all its weight against the pinned calf of his scrawny leg. But through his blinding agony, Roy still managed to see his chance and seize it. The next time the animal pushed against the glass, he readied himself. When the thing let go and prepared to push again, Roy shoved against the door with his right foot and jerked his left leg free, so when the beast pushed against the door again, it slammed closed and latched in place.

Roy thumped the lock with his bloody hand, and then turned and slid quickly and painfully to the other side of the cab, using his feet to scoot himself across the well-worn fabric of the bench seat. He put his back against the passenger door without ever taking his eyes off the behemoth.

Another roar, angry and loud.

Then, the animal changed strategy, pushing against the door in rhythmic waves, rocking the truck back and forth as if trying to tip it over. Was the son of a bitch smart enough to know it could tip the vehicle over? It sure seemed that way.

"Go away, you ugly bastard," Roy shouted, feeling much braver now that there was a barrier between him and the wild animal.

He wondered where the hell the cops were. He had called them hours ago. They should be here by now. But it was no surprise that they hadn't arrived yet. That was par for the course in this neck of the woods. People often died waiting on the police or an ambulance to get to them. While Roy understood that the local emergency crews had a lot of area to cover and not a lot of manpower, he sometimes wondered if they ever got in a hurry at all to get to the folks who needed their help.

This was one of those times.

And where the hell was Luke and Tom? Roy had never wanted to see their ugly mugs more than he did at that moment.

Dying would suck. Dying alone would suck even more.

The creature looked Roy straight in the eyes and roared again, as if promising to get to him no matter what. Then, it dropped down on all four legs and disappeared from Roy's line of sight.

No longer staring into the eyes of the raging monster or its gaping maw, Roy relaxed, letting his head fall back against the passenger window as he breathed a sigh of relief. He didn't make the mistake of fooling himself into thinking the thing was gone—he'd already made that mistake once—but he felt he could safely relax a little because it was out there, and he was in here, inside the cab of the truck, out of the reach of those frighteningly long and unimaginably sharp claws that had already done so much damage to Roy's thin body. He was safe and sound in the truck, surrounded by comforting steel, while the beast was outside trying to figure out how to get to him.

It's just an animal, Roy told himself. It's nowhere near as smart as a human. It was dumb, really. Damn near stupid. Besides, the police would be here soon and would have the thing shot before it could figure out a way to get to him.

The window in the passenger door busted behind Roy's head, showering him with shards of glass and shattering all his illusions of safety and superiority.

chapter **EIGHTEEN**

The thought had crossed Luke's mind to take the vehicle. It would be a hell of a lot easier than walking all the way back to Tom and then to Roy back at the truck, but there was a whole slew of problems with that idea.

For one, driving the vehicle would only allow him to travel by road. He had no idea where he was, where the logging road lead, or how to get back to Tom or to Roy any way other than the way he'd come. He could find his way back through the forest, retracing his steps, but he'd never find them if he went off in another direction.

The second problem was that he didn't have the keys. They weren't in the ignition, and even if the lower half of the dead driver had been left behind by the animal, Luke sure as hell wasn't about to go searching through the man's pockets in the hopes that he might have put the keys in there.

A third problem was that taking the truck would be stealing. Technically, it would be borrowing because Luke had no intentions whatsoever of keeping it. He simply needed a quick way to get back to his friends. But in the eyes of the law, and most assuredly in the eyes of the truck's owner, it would be stealing. And Luke Davis— a.k.a. James L., a.k.a. Whistlepig, a.k.a. Bloodhound—was a lot of things, but he wasn't a thief.

Then, of course, there was the mess in the cab of the truck. Even if he had the keys, a clearly-marked map that would take him directly to where he wanted to go, and the owner's written permission, there was no way in hell that he was going to get in and drive that thing. Not if it meant having to sit on a pile of blood and viscera.

That left him with only two viable options.

One, he could walk back. But that would take a lot of time on a night when time was in short supply.

Or two, he could take the ATV. It would allow him to follow the same route back to Tom and Roy that he had taken to get to the campsite. It would be faster. Easier. And bonus, the keys were in it.

Of course, that option would still leave him with the moral dilemma of having stolen it, but he supposed that with all things considered, it was something he had to do. He'd deal with the consequences later. For now, there was too much at stake for him to get caught up on a technicality. He would explain his actions later, to both the cops and the owners of the ATV, assuming they were alive to ask questions and demand answers. But for now, he had to do what he had to do.

"Look at you, you beautiful thing," he said as he climbed on-to the four-wheeler. He didn't see a helmet, but safety wasn't exactly his top priority at the moment. He settled onto the machine and reached for the keys, which dangled from the ignition as if they'd been placed there just for him.

A voice, small and scared, said, "Mister?"

Luke looked around but saw no one. He said, "Yes?"

A young boy crawled out from beneath the old camper. He stood, staring at Luke with frightened eyes and tear-stained cheeks.

"Where is everyone?" Luke asked, feeling certain he already knew the answer.

The boy shrugged.

Luke nodded. It was probably for the best that the kid didn't know.

"What happened here?" Again, asking a question he already knew the answer to.

Another shrug.

"I'm, uh...I'm going to borrow this," Luke said, indicating the ATV. When the kid didn't say anything, Luke asked, "Is it yours?"

A slight shake of the head.

"Your dad's?"

More head shaking.

"Well I'll make sure you get it back. I promise."

The boy stared at Luke, not moving. Not speaking. He stood still, his arms hanging limp at his sides.

Luke looked at the kid, wondering what he should do with him. He didn't know for sure that all the other people in the camp were dead, but he knew he couldn't leave the kid there and just assume there was someone to take care of him because if he was wrong, it would mean certain death for the little guy. Besides, Luke felt sure that if anyone else at the camp was alive, they would've made their presence known by now.

Looking at the kid, Luke asked, "What's your name?"

"Denny."

"How old are you?"

"Seven."

"Seven, huh? So I assume this is your truck?" Luke said with a forced smile. It was a lame joke in a pathetic attempt to put the kid at ease. When he saw the joke didn't land, Luke grew serious. "Denny, I'm Luke. Do you want to come with me?"

The boy looked unsure of what he should do. His parents had no doubt talked to him about the danger of strangers and how he shouldn't talk to them and how he should certainly never go anywhere with them when they asked. Now here he was, being asked to go with a total stranger further into the woods in the middle of the night in the wake of a traumatic event. He was scared and confused, as any child would—and honestly should—be.

He tried to make the kid relax with some idle chit chat. "I came out here with my friends Roy and Tom."

A blank stare.

"Tom and Roy were deer hunting. Tom shot this big ol' deer, but it ran off. They couldn't find it, so they came to my house and picked me up so I could find it for them." He made no mention of the decision to forget the deer and instead hunt for the thing that had

109

killed a little girl about Denny's age. He wanted to put the boy at ease, not scar him for life. "You want to know why they came to get me?"

The boy blinked.

"Because they call me Bloodhound Luke. It's because I'm really good at tracking animals." Luke expected the boy to smile at the silly moniker, but he didn't. "Do you have a nickname? Something the other kids call you? Or maybe your parents?"

"Scooter," the boy said, barely above a whisper.

"Scooter, huh? Why do they call you that?"

"I used to scoot," he mumbled.

"Oh yeah?" Luke pretended to be far more interested in the boy's nickname than he really was, showing feigned excitement as if that was the most peculiar and fascinating thing he'd ever heard. It seemed to help the boy warm up to him.

"When I was a baby, I didn't crawl. I scooted on the floor. My dad called me Scooter. Then everybody started calling me that."

"Well that's a much better name than mine. You want to trade? I'll be Scooter and you can be Bloodhound Luke?"

Denny shook his head.

"Not even for a little while?"

More head shaking. "No."

"Why not?"

"Because I'm not Luke. I'm Scooter."

Luke nodded. "That's a very good reason. Okay, Scooter. How about you and I head back to where my friends are?"

Denny looked uncertain about going with Luke.

To reassure the boy, Luke said, "My friend Roy called the Sheriff. The cops are on their way. Actually," he glanced at his watch, "they're probably already here. It's been long enough since he made the call. I'm going to meet them now. I think you should come with me."

Denny still seemed unsure.

Luke said, "I don't think it's safe for you to stay here by yourself."

The boy didn't move.

"You know, I have a daughter named Hope. You remind me of her." The boy didn't remind Luke of Hope in any way, but he

110

wanted to let the kid know that he had a child of his own and there-fore was harmless and trustworthy.

This seemed to work, as the boy walked slowly toward Luke.

"You out here deer hunting?" Luke asked, trying to keep the boy's mind off the horrors he must have experienced and the fear he was surely feeling.

"No," the boy mumbled.

Luke nodded, wondering what else they could possibly be doing out here if not hunting. In the summer, folks camped pretty much everywhere. At the river. At the lake. In the woods. But in the winter, the only people willing to brave the cold weather to sleep outside in tiny tin boxes were hunters. Especially when they were camping in the woods. If you were going to camp for reasons other than hunting, you wouldn't do it in the middle of nowhere. You'd do it at the lake or the river, where there were things to see and do. In the forest, the only thing to do other than hunt was watch the trees grow.

"Where you from?" Luke asked, hoping that if he asked enough questions, he would eventually land on an ice-breaker that got the kid talking.

"Poplar Bluff."

"Have you camped out here before?"

"No."

"Do you have any brothers or sisters?"

"No."

This kid was quite the conversationalist. "An only child, huh? That must be nice. You don't have to share your toys. Nobody to fight with."

Denny said nothing.

"Why don't you hop on?"

Denny made no move to get on the ATV.

"I won't let anything happen to you. I promise."

After weighing the words of the stranger, the boy decided he could trust him. He walked slowly toward the four-wheeler, keeping his eyes on Luke as if he expected him to lunge forward and grab him. Or maybe he was afraid Luke would take off and leave him alone again.

When the kid was settled on the seat behind him, Luke turned his head and spoke over his shoulder. "Hang on to my waist, Scooter." Luke felt the boy's arms wrap around him, those little hands clenching together over his abdomen.

He started the ATV, put it in gear, and accelerated, happy to have a means of transportation other than his aching feet that would carry him back to the truck, then to civilization, and eventually to Susan, who better have saved him several slices of meatloaf because his stomach was rumbling with hunger.

chapter **NINETEEN**

Before Roy had a chance to push himself away from the door, he felt those long, sharp claws sink deep into his right shoulder. He screamed. He cussed. And then he wriggled out of the monster's reach, away from those damn claws, and jumped to the other side of the bench seat. His heart was racing, which was exactly what he didn't want to happen. He couldn't afford for it to happen because the faster his heart beat, the faster it pumped blood out of his many wounds. Which meant the faster he would bleed to death. And he was already feeling a couple pints low.

He leaned against the driver side door and stared at the creature, who seemed furious at having to work for its next meal.

The animal hooked its claws over the top of the passenger door and began pulling, trying to rip the thing off its hinges.

"Oh shit," Roy said. He tried to recall all he had learned about wild animals throughout the years, about what to do if he was ever unlucky enough to encounter an angry one. He couldn't remember if he was supposed to make loud noises or be quiet, make himself appear big or curl up into a ball, or if he should play dead. It didn't help matters any that he still wasn't sure what the thing was. All he knew for sure was it wasn't a bigfoot, and it wasn't a chop-peecobbree.

He suddenly wished he hadn't drunk all those beers. He needed a clear head but his was fuzzy. And it wasn't all due to blood loss, though that certainly factored into the equation.

The animal roared and yanked hard on the door. The metal crunched, giving way under the pressure. A few more pulls like that and the door would break free, leaving nothing standing between Roy and the monster.

"Go away, you bastard," he shouted, his voice barely audible over the animal's grunts and the sound of metal creaking under the strain of the animal's jerks and tugs.

He glanced to his right and saw the beast heave on the door. The top half of it bent outward, away from the truck's frame.

The way Roy saw it, he only had a few options, and none of them were appealing.

He could stay in the cab of the truck and wait for the door to give way—which it inevitably would—and for the animal to gain entry. Which would also inevitably happen. Then, when it climbed inside with him, he could try to wrestle with it, but in the end, he would lose. So long, Roy. It was fun while it lasted.

Or he could get out of the truck and run, but he wouldn't make it far in his condition. He had a sprained ankle, an injured calf, deep gouges in his back, puncture wounds in his shoulder, and his right side was shredded to shit. And though the pain and adrenaline pushed away the buzz he'd had and cleared his mind a bit, the blood loss fogged it right back up and made him feel drunker than he had been before. He wouldn't be able to run far before he became disoriented and got lost, or worse, fell. Then, goodbye, Roy. Hope you enjoyed the ride.

Or he could get out of the truck and hide underneath it. It was a move that had worked once already and might just work again. He saw this as his best course of action. It would keep him at the truck, which was where Luke and Tom would be returning to and what the Sheriff's Deputies would use to locate them. It would also offer him at least some sort of protection against the wild animal. Plus, it would require very little physical exertion on his part.

The door broke loose of the frame. The animal fell backward, landing on its ass, holding the detached door in its giant paws.

Roy saw his chance and took it. He opened the door and slid out, falling onto the ground as quietly as possible. He didn't bother to shut the door because he didn't want to attract the animal's attention. He rolled underneath the truck, lined himself up down the center of the vehicle, and laid perfectly still.

Roy watched the animal get to its feet from his place beneath the truck, trying to keep his breathing shallow. He saw it stand, watched as its legs disappeared as it climbed up into the cab of the truck. The shocks creaked as the additional weight squatted the body of the vehicle down. Roy was in no danger of being crushed, but just knowing that thing was above him made him nervous all the same.

He considered running, but Roy reminded himself that he was in no shape to do anything other than stay where he was and lie still. So that's what he did, though it took considerable effort to fight his instincts and remain so close to the monster.

As a child, Roy's parents had dragged him to church every Sunday morning and again in the evening, both times against his will. That was fifty-two weeks a year that he'd had to sit on the wooden pew, arms folded over his small chest, angry that he'd been forced to go to services when he would've much rather stayed home and done almost anything else. He could've played. He could've read his comic books for the thousandth time. He could've tossed the ball around with the fellas. He could've done anything except get dressed up in his nicest and most uncomfortable clothes and listen as the preacher yelled from the pulpit about how he was failing to please his god. When Roy had complained to his mother about how bored he was at church, she'd told him that if he was bored, he could keep himself occupied by praying, which is what he was supposed to be doing anyway. He protested, telling her he didn't want to pray. Then, when she forced him to close his eyes and bow his head, he did as he was told. But he still didn't pray. He thought of other things, anything he could conjure up in his young mind. But, mostly out of sheer spite, Roy refused to pray.

But that was then.

Now, Roy was all too eager to squeeze his eyes closed and speak passionately to a deity he hadn't talked to in a long time.

Above him, the beast wreaked havoc on Tom's truck. Plastic snapped. Glass shattered. The horn blared. Pieces of metal popped. Occasionally, something flew out of the vehicle, landing on the ground several feet away from where Roy laid praying. Buttons and knobs and other various portions of a truck that would most likely never run again after this night.

Once there was nothing left in the cab to destroy, the animal jumped out of the truck. The sound of the shocks creaking alerted Roy to this fact, cutting his prayer short. His eyes opened, his breath caught in his lungs. If the animal found him—and he assumed it would since it had a heightened sense of smell and Roy reeked of blood and alcohol and nicotine and cold sweat—and it figured out a way to get to him, his night would end horribly.

When he thought of the last words he had spoken to his wife, *why are you a bitch*, he realized that he didn't want the night—or his life—to end that way. If he managed to survive for no other reason and only long enough to do one thing, it would be to tell Linda how sorry he was.

And not just for calling her a bitch.

chapter **TWENTY**

Luke maneuvered the ATV through the forest, carefully driving over rocks and roots while dodging fallen trees and downed limbs. He didn't drive too fast for fear that Denny would fall off the back, but he didn't want to drive too slowly because he wanted to get back to Tom so they could get the hell out of these woods and go home.

When Luke agreed to come out with Tom and Roy, he damn sure hadn't expected the night go like it had. He figured they'd find the deer Tom had shot and be back home within a couple hours, at most. He never expected to be trudging around the woods in the farthest corners of the county in the wee hours of the morning, exhausted and frozen, scared of both finding and not finding an animal that was racking up a body count that was sure to rival that of the most prolific of serial killers. And now he was in charge of a stranger's kid.

It was funny how life turned out sometimes.

Over his shoulder, Luke asked, "You okay back there, Scooter?"

Denny answered, "Yeah. But I need to pee."

"What?" The boy was small and had a voice to match, making it nearly impossible for Luke to hear him over the roar of the engine.

Raising his voice, Denny repeated, "I have to pee."

"Oh. Okay." Luke stopped the four-wheeler and killed the motor. He needed the silence to be able to hear if something was about to attack them. When he felt Denny hop off the back, Luke said, "Stay where I can see you."

The boy did as he was told, walking toward the front of the ATV where the headlight gave Luke a clear view of him.

Looking at the kid now, Luke noticed just how thin he was. It wasn't difficult to discern as he wasn't dressed for the cold weather. Instead of a coat, he wore a jacket. Beneath that, a t-shirt. He had on jeans, dirty and sporting holes in the knees. On his feet were tennis shoes. Nothing about the kid's attire said he was prepared to camp in the cold weather. Deer hunters, even those that sat around the campfire in the evening, wore overalls, coveralls, and several layers of thick clothing underneath to keep warm. And those were grown men. While kids could handle cold weather better than adults, they were more susceptible to frostbite and hypothermia. This kid's parents must be—or rather must have been—negligent to bring him out there wearing nothing other than what he was wearing. If Luke hadn't come along and found him, Denny would've frozen to death before daybreak.

"Are you cold?" he asked the boy, who stood with his back to him, peeing.

"No," Denny replied. He kept his back to Luke as he did his business, his head lowered as he focused on the job at hand.

Meanwhile, Luke glanced around in all directions to be sure nothing was creeping up on them. When he saw nothing, he took out his can of tobacco, pinched a bit between his fingers, and placed it in his mouth. As he returned the can to his pocket, Denny turned and walked back to the ATV.

"Are you sure you're not cold?" Luke asked.

"I'm sure," the boy said quietly.

"Didn't you bring anything warmer with you? Like a coat?"

Denny hung his head, shook it slightly.

Then it occurred to Luke that maybe the kid's parents couldn't afford to buy him appropriate hunting clothes. He thought of the condition of the camper and the scant items around the camp site. Suddenly, Luke felt horrible for not thinking of this earlier.

"Here," Luke said, taking off his coat and handing it to the boy. "Wear this. I know you said you're not cold, but I'm just going to keep thinking that you are, so it'll make me feel better if you wear it."

Denny took the coat from Luke and pulled it on slowly, slipping his tiny arms into the large sleeves. The thing swallowed him whole, hanging down past his knees. He struggled to pull the sleeves up and expose his hands, so Luke offered his help, rolling the cuffs up until the kid's little fists were visible.

"And here," he added, pulling gloves from the pockets of the coat and sliding them on Denny's hands. Fortunately, they were the kind with the adjustable Velcro strap on the back of the wrist, allowing him to tighten the gloves and keep them from falling off the kid's tiny hands. "There you go. That ought to keep you warm."

Denny held up his hands, inspecting the thick gloves that were way too big. "Thanks," he said. He almost smiled.

"Okay, Scooter. Let's get going."

Once they were settled on the ATV, Luke turned the key and pushed the button, cranking the engine to life. He turned his head and spit as Denny's arms slid around his waist. Then, he took off in search of Tom, wondering about the little boy who sat behind him.

chapter **TWENTY-ONE**

Tom laid on the ground, waiting and hoping for the pain to pass as the cold seeped through his clothing. Though his agony sheltered him from the chill, keeping him warm enough to not feel it, it registered in his bones.

His chest felt constricted and heavy, as if it was cramped tightly in a gnarly spasm that just wouldn't go away. Oddly, his left arm was numb and aching at the same time. It seemed he was in a real pickle. Tom had often wondered what a heart attack would feel like. He'd long suspected that he would experience at least one coronary episode in his lifetime, and he wanted to know what to expect when the time came. As it turned out, it felt a hell of a lot worse than he'd ever imagined.

Despite his agony, all he could really think about was how he was lying in a puddle of his own vomit, consisting mostly of partially digested beef jerky and soda. Well, that and what his girlfriend would do if he died.

Most likely, she would mourn him for a month. Maybe two. But then she'd move on, find another man to fill his role in her life.

It saddened him to think about it, but he had always known that their relationship meant more to him than it did to her. That was the nature of the beast when you dated a much younger woman with a proven track record for bed hopping.

Had Tom not divorced his wife—or rather, had she not divorced him—his thoughts would've been wildly different as he laid on the ground having his heart attack. He could've thought about how his poor wife would miss him and mourn his passing for years to come, if not for the rest of her life. He could've thought about what his children would do and how they would provide comfort for their widowed mother. He could've been grateful for having all his affairs in order before he died, his life insurance paid up, his burial paid for. He could've spent his last minutes on this earth reflecting on a life well-lived, on all the good times he'd had with his family and all the wonderful memories they'd made together throughout the years. He could've been at peace with himself and with all the decisions he'd made in his lifetime. That's the way it was for some people. But that wasn't how things had played out for Tom Wilkins.

Instead of dying on the forest floor, comforted by the good life he'd lived and the knowledge that he was loved by the family he'd created, he was forced to wallow in his misery alone, consoled only by the thought that it would all be over soon.

And it was all his fault.

He'd once shared a relatively nice four-bedroom house with his wife and kids. They'd spent their evenings gathered around the television, eating dinner and watching sitcoms and movies together like a real family. Their weekends had been spent driving through the park, skipping rocks at the river, taking pontoons out on Clearwater Lake, and barbecuing with their friends. The kids had had ball games to attend, baseball and basketball and soccer and volleyball. They went to Spring Fever Day together, walking up and down Main Street, eating and buying things they didn't need from the booths along the way. They'd driven to town every fourth of July and watched the city's fireworks display before grabbing a pizza and heading home to play board games and eat. But all good things had to come to an end.

Like his marriage.

And his life.

Tom first began to notice that his wife wasn't as interested in doing things with him as she used to be when she no longer wanted to go on those rides through the park or to skip rocks along the banks of Current River. She started out using the excuses of having a headache or being too tired to go. Then, she either ran out of excuses to use or simply stopped trying to come up with them. She would merely say she didn't want to go. "You and the kids go," she'd say. "I'll just stay here and read a book or sew or something." He had shrugged and went without her, never thinking that it was only the beginning of her pulling away from him.

The beginning of the end of their life together.

He was never sure whether the kids had simply picked up on their contention or if his wife had poisoned them against him, but it wasn't long until they no longer wanted to do those things with him either.

A rift formed between Tom and his wife and his kids that grew wider every day. They no longer sat around the TV as a family. They no longer talked. When they did speak to each other, it was in short, tense sentences. But even that was cordial compared to the arguments that followed. He couldn't ask what was for dinner without a fight erupting that would last for hours. The same thing would happen when she asked him where he was going when he left to hang out at the bar and drink his woes away. Eventually, they stopped asking each other anything.

A year after that, she left him and took the kids with her.

It turned out to be the best thing that could've happened to either of them, though. They got along much better after the divorce was finalized. She moved into a smaller house with the kids, and Tom moved into an old mobile home close to his dad. The kids came over whenever they wanted to be with him. And his relationship with his wife had actually improved. They were friends again. No more arguing. No more fighting. No more tension.

For a while after their split, Tom had enjoyed the silence that came with his newfound bachelorhood. But that wore off rather quickly, and he soon found himself lonely. He ate his frustration for a while, and then he started to spend more and more time at the bar. He didn't always drink, but he did always eat. Tom had always found bar food, for whatever reason, to be delicious. The burgers.

The sandwiches. The pizzas. All were irresistible. And he had the body to prove it.

It was there, at the bar, that he had met her. She came in one night with a group of other women, but she left with him. She was vastly different than his wife, which was both a good and a bad thing. She wasn't his type by any means. In fact, she was the complete opposite of his type. She was young, which meant she knew nothing about anything. She was far too thin, and Tom liked his women to have curves. Something to hold onto and provide softness and comfort. She had a loud voice and an even louder laugh. She was inconsiderate and selfish. Abrasive and crass. And oftentimes, she was just downright inappropriate. Tom had decided early on in their relationship that he would never bring her around his friends. And he sure as hell wouldn't introduce her to his kids. She was a secret he kept from everybody he knew.

Especially Roy.

Tom had been seeing Destiny for a few months before he found out that she'd been with Roy. He knew his friend had cheated on his wife, but he hadn't known who he'd cheated on her with. When Destiny felt the need to run down the rather long list of men she'd been with, Tom's ears had perked up at the mention of Roy. He kept it to himself, though. He didn't tell her that he knew Roy. She was a part of his life that he didn't want to share with anyone else. And he had a feeling that if she knew he and Roy were friends, it would lead to problems. She would somehow use that against him. She gave off a vibe that hit Tom wrong and made him feel that Destiny was nothing but trouble.

Yet, he didn't stop seeing her.

It wasn't her winning personality that kept him going back because she didn't have one.

It wasn't her charm because she didn't possess any.

It wasn't her wit because she was slower than cold molasses.

It wasn't her lovemaking skills because Tom had had better times with his own hand than he'd had with her.

And it certainly wasn't her intellect because she had once asked him if Canada was a state. And then, when he'd told her no, she wanted to know why not.

He wasn't sure exactly what it was that kept him going back to her, but he figured it had something to do with the companionship.

She was someone to be with, someone to talk to. Someone to be there so he didn't have to be alone. He was closing in on fifty years old. He was obese. He was out of shape. And he was broke. The entirety of his earthly possessions added up to less than a grand. His chances of landing someone better than Destiny at this point in his life were slim to none. So he did what all divorced, middle-aged, overweight men did. He took what he could get.

His girlfriend annoyed him. She embarrassed him. To be with her, he had to sneak around and lie to his friends and family, but he figured as long as the honey was worth the sting, he would keep seeing her.

Tom made a fist, then opened his hand and wiggled his fingers, trying to determine if the pain was easing or was still the same. He wasn't sure.

He then wondered what Destiny was doing right then. Probably something stupid, like watching cartoons. His kids had outgrown it, but his girlfriend hadn't. Just as he realized how stupid the whole situation was, he heard something in the woods. It grew closer and closer to him. And it was fast.

So fast.

chapter **TWENTY-TWO**

Roy had been hiding under the truck for what felt like an eternity. It couldn't have been more than half an hour, maybe forty-five minutes, but with the adrenaline pumping and the beast trying to get to him, it felt longer. Much longer. He squeezed his eyes shut, praying the damn thing would give up and go away. He wasn't sure how much longer he could take it.

He flinched when one of the tires popped, the back left one. The sound of it echoed under the truck, making every muscle in Roy's body stiffen. The act intensified the pain in the wounds on his back and side.

Another tire popped, on the back right side. The ass end of the truck dropped down half a foot or more. Roy tasted a new flavor of fear then as he considered the possibility that he might be crushed under the weight of the heavy vehicle.

A minute passed. Then one of the front tires popped. Then the other. How the hell did the animal know to do that, he wondered. Surely, it didn't *know* to do that. It had to be a fluke. It must have accidentally punctured the rubber with its teeth or claws.

But four times?

When the last tire popped, the truck creaked and dropped again, stopping just before it crushed Roy, leaving no more than an inch between the back of his skull and the bottom of the truck. He suddenly felt claustrophobic, like he was trapped and couldn't breathe.

Like he was in a coffin.

On the driver's side of the truck, the animal stuck its snout under the truck and chuffed, sending a chill crawling down Roy's spine. His bladder threatened to release itself into his pants.

The beast then began to paw at the dirt, using those long claws to tear through the frozen earth in a frenzied and desperate attempt to get to Roy. He had hoped it would forget about him, or at least fail to find him and give up and go away. Instead, it had focused on him and became determined to get under the truck. No doubt, to finish what it had started earlier and rip the rest of his body to shreds.

The damn thing probably smelled Roy's blood, which flowed freely from his body. He felt it oozing out between his fingers, running down his side, and falling to the ground. Though he couldn't see it, Roy assumed a puddle had accumulated and spilled out from under the vehicle, leaving a trail that led the bastard directly to him.

Damn the luck.

Roy watched as the creature continued to dig, wondering what he would do if it began to crawl under the truck with him. Other than piss himself, that is. He didn't have the strength to fight it. He didn't have the stamina to run from it. He didn't even think he had the smarts required to outwit it.

He was a sitting duck.

When the fear got the better of him, Roy grabbed a fistful of bloody dirt and threw it at the animal's face, filling its eyes and snout with the grit.

It jumped back, retreating with a whimper, pawing at its eyes and shaking its head. Then the thing roared, loud and long and angry.

Suddenly, just as Roy's bladder spilled its warm contents into his underwear, the thing crammed its face into the narrow opening beneath the truck, less than two feet away from Roy's head, and roared. The sound boomed in the small space beneath the truck, striking Roy's ears hard and vibrating his eardrums nearly to the point of rupturing.

He'd angered it, which was precisely what he didn't want to happen.

The animal continued to roar.

Roy yelled, "Go away!"

When it finally stopping roaring, it started digging again, working in a fevered frenzy to get to the food that was putting up a fight.

Roy watched in horror for a moment before kicking into action. He was in no shape to run, but he couldn't stay put. He quickly scooted to the side of the truck opposite the creature, keeping his eyes on the thing as he went. Every movement sent fresh waves of agony rolling through Roy's body, but it would be nothing compared to the pain he would experience if he didn't move at all.

He thought of standing up to run away from the truck, but the animal might see him, so he remained flat on the ground, pulling himself forward with his arms, dragging himself across the frozen earth. He had no plan, no idea of what the hell he was going to do or how he would do it. He was thinking on the fly, his fuzzy mind racing as fast as it could.

Where the hell was Luke and Tom?

And for the love of god, where were the cops?

Gravel crunched behind him.

A grunt.

A growl.

A snort.

Roy didn't need to look to know that the damn thing was behind him.

127

chapter **TWENTY-THREE**

Tom used every bit of strength he had to push himself up from the ground and return to the downed tree from which he'd fallen, keeping his left arm held tightly against his chest all the while.

He then watched as the man sprang from a cluster of trees and ran west, following the path Luke had taken earlier after promising to return soon. Tom looked on as the stranger jumped and ducked and dodged his way through the forest, a rifle gripped tightly in both hands.

Not wanting to be mistaken for the animal and shot, he decided to say something to let the guy know he was there.

"Hey," Tom yelled.

The man turned mid-stride and threw up his rifle, locking his sights on Tom with lightning-fast speed and deadly accuracy as he landed solidly on both feet. "Who's that?" he asked.

"Name's Tom. Who are you?" Tom reached up and clicked on his headlamp. It shined in the man's direction, but from that distance and with the gun in the way, Tom couldn't see the stranger's face.

The man walked toward Tom without lowering his weapon or saying a word.

"I said who are you?" Tom repeated, unsettled at the man's military-like movements and silence. And of course, at the barrel of the gun that remained aimed directly at his head.

"Tom who?" the stranger asked, his voice taking on an odd and suspicious tone.

"Tom Wilkins. What'd you say your name was?" He squeezed his left arm against his chest, willing his heart to continue pumping.

"I didn't."

"So I noticed." A chill slithered down Tom's spine. There was something weird about this guy. Why wouldn't he tell him his name? And why the hell wouldn't he lower that rifle?

"What are you doing out here?" the man asked. Or, more accurately, demanded.

"Well right now, I'm trying not to die." Tom tried to smile, but it came out a wince as his heart cramped in his chest. "I'm pretty sure I'm havin' a heart attack."

"Is that so?" The man finally lowered his gun, allowing the glow of Tom's flashlight to illuminate his face.

"Hey," Tom said. "It's you."

"Yeah. It's me." John Ramshaw looked around the area and asked, "Where's your friend?"

"I don't know."

"What do you mean you don't know?" His tone suggested more than casual curiosity.

Tom looked at him, wondering why he was so interested in Luke's whereabouts. He replied, "I mean I'm not sure where he is. You have any luck findin' it?"

"Finding what?"

"Findin' what? Findin' the animal. Isn't that what you came out here to do?"

"Oh yeah. Yeah. No, I ain't had no luck." He sounded preoccupied, like his mind was somewhere else. He looked around as if he was expecting someone. Luke perhaps? Or someone else? Had he called for help too?

Tom squeezed his eyes closed, fighting through a bolt of pain and a wave of nausea. He wondered how much longer he would last without some sort of medical intervention. Not long, surely.

Opening his eyes again, Tom asked, "Hey, you wouldn't happen to have a vehicle out here, would ya? Maybe an ATV? A four-wheeler or a side-by-side? Maybe one of them little mini trucks? Fuck, at this point, I'd settle for a damn semi."

"No. Why? What'd you hear?" John was jumpy. Oddly suspicious of everything Tom said.

"Nothing. I just thought if you had somethin' I could borrow to get me back to my truck, I might make it to a hospital in time. And if I don't make it all the way to the hospital before I konk out, at least it'll be easier for them to collect my bones." He offered a weak smile, but it was met with a stony stare.

Seeing that John wasn't going to offer any assistance, Tom said, "Alright then. I guess I could walk..." He stood slowly, his body protesting every move he made. His head swam, his vision darkened. His mouth filled with saliva, and his stomach rolled. "I don't feel so gooooo..." Tom collapsed onto the ground, leaving John Ramshaw standing over his unconscious body.

chapter **TWENTY-FOUR**

Luke stopped the ATV and killed the engine. He jumped off the machine, careful to not kick Denny in the face in the process. He ran to where Tom sat with his back against a tree, arms pulled behind him and bound by ropes that wrapped around the trunk, and his head hung down. Luke dropped to his knees and began tugging at the ropes that bound his friend. "Who did this to you?" he asked.

Tom didn't respond. Luke wasn't even sure the man was awake. He would find that out later, after he'd freed his hands and feet.

The ropes were pulled taut, the knots firm in their place. Luke pulled out his pocketknife and began sawing through the thick fibers, desperate to rid his friend of his bonds. As he worked, he wondered who had done this and why.

Tom moaned.

Luke asked, "Tom? What happened? Who did this to you?"

Another moan.

The ropes were dense. Using a small pocketknife to saw through them seemed like a fool's errand. And though Luke worked fervently, the job was slow going.

"I'm hurrying, buddy," he told Tom. "Can you hear me?"

"Yeah," Tom mumbled. "Can you hear me?"

"Of course. What happened?"

"John."

"John? Who the hell's John?"

"Ramshaw."

"John Ramshaw? The guy from before? The little girl's uncle?"

Tom nodded weakly. "He came back."

Luke continued to cut the ropes, his mind racing as to what John Ramshaw had to do with Tom being bound to a tree.

"Tied me up," Tom added.

"Why?"

Shaking his head, Tom said, "I don't know. I blacked out. Woke up as he finished tyin' my hands. He took off. I blacked out again."

"Did he hit you over the head or something?" Luke cut through the last of the rope, pulled it free of Tom's hands, and tossed it aside.

"No."

"Then why did you black out?"

"Pain."

"What hurts?"

"My heart."

"Because you missed me?" Luke asked with a smile.

Tom grinned. "You wish."

Turning serious, Luke asked, "Are you having a heart attack?"

"Yeah."

"Goddamn it, Tom. I knew this was gonna happen."

"Save the lecture for the funeral."

"There's not going to be a funeral. You can die on your own time. We're going to get you to the hospital. Now come on." Luke stood. He then bent down to help Tom get to his feet.

"I don't think I can make it back. It's too far."

"Well isn't this your lucky day?"

132

"Not yet, it's not."

"I've got some wheels."

Luke nodded his head in the direction of the ATV. Tom looked past Luke, to where Denny sat on the four-wheeler.

"You did it wrong," Tom said, struggling to his feet. "You're supposed to beat the kid up and then take his ride. Not take the ride and the kid."

"I found the wheels. And the kid."

"You found a kid? In the woods? Alone?"

"Well, he's alone now. But there were others."

Tom and Luke exchanged a quick glance.

"The creature?" Tom asked.

"Yeah. It was messy."

Looking over at Denny, Tom asked, "How is he?"

Luke shrugged and said, "Considering the things he must've seen and experienced tonight, I'd say he's doing pretty good. Scared. But good."

Tom slapped one hand onto Luke's shoulder. "Glory hog. Always the hero."

"Not always," Luke said grimly, thinking that if he didn't get Tom to a hospital soon, he'd lose his friend forever and would never be able to forgive himself for letting this happen.

The men walked to the ATV, Tom leaning heavily on Luke who struggled to support the additional weight. Denny watched them both, looking even smaller than he really was inside the over-sized clothing.

"How are we gonna do this?" Tom asked, struggling to breathe.

"Do you think you can drive this thing?"

Tom thought for a moment before answering, "Well hell yes. I've been drivin' since I was ten. Legally since I was eighteen. Trucks, cars, vans, tractors. You name it, I can drive it."

"I meant can you drive it without passing out and crashing the damn thing?"

"Oh, well, then no."

"That's what I thought. Okay. Um..." Luke studied the seat. There was no way that it would accommodate Luke, Denny, and a man of Tom's size. But Tom needed it more than Luke. As did Denny. Luke looked at the boy and asked, "Can you drive it?"

The boy shrugged.

"Haven't you driven it before?"

Denny shook his head.

"Have you ever driven any four-wheeler?"

This time, the kid nodded.

"Okay. Well they're pretty much all the same. Do you think you can drive it out of here? Get Tom back to his truck if he tells you which way to go?"

Denny nodded again. He looked nervous and unsure of himself, but there was no other choice. The only one of the three of them that could chance being left behind was Luke. Tom needed to get to a hospital immediately or he would die, and Denny needed to get to somewhere warm before he suffered frostbite or hypothermia. Luke wasn't sure how long he'd been exposed to the cold, but he was small, and it wouldn't take long for him to succumb to the low temperature.

Luke helped Tom get on the back of the machine. He then started the ATV and gave Denny a crash course in how to operate it.

"Now," he said to the boy, "just listen to Tom. He'll tell you which way to go. If he passes out and slumps forward, just keep driving. Try to get to the truck. If he falls off the back..." He looked at Tom, who was looking worse by the minute. There would be no way for the boy to help Tom get back on the four-wheeler if he fell off. It had taken a lot for Luke to do it, and he was a grown man. Shrugging, Luke said, "I don't know. If he falls off, just keep going, I guess. Try to get to the truck. Roy is there. You can stay in the truck while he takes the four-wheeler back to get Tom. Just tell Roy how to get to him. Think you can handle it?"

Denny nodded.

"Good. Now go as quickly as possible, but be careful. The last thing I need is for you to wreck this thing and hurt yourself." To Tom he said, "You and Roy take Denny with you and go on to the hospital when you get back to the truck. I'll catch a ride with the cops. Don't wait on me. Get your ass to the hospital. You hear me?"

"Yeah, yeah."

"Don't 'yeah, yeah' me. You've been doing that for too long as it is, which is why you're in this mess now. Now get going. And be care—"

The blow came hard and fast, striking the right side of Luke's head. He dropped like a stone, falling where he stood.

"Where y'all runnin' off to?"

Luke rolled over onto his back and looked up at John Ramshaw, who stood over him, holding his rifle in both hands. He'd used the butt of it to hit Luke, and all Luke could think about right then was how far he wanted to ram it up the guy's ass.

"You ain't goin' nowhere," he said to Tom. And then to Denny, he added, "And you for damn sure ain't goin' nowhere."

With his head pounding, Luke tried to figure out how John knew Denny. And why didn't he want him to go anywhere?

When John let go of the rifle with his right hand and reached out to grab the kid, Luke screamed for Denny to go while kicking his leg out and up, planting his foot directly in the son of a bitch's crotch.

John doubled over, moaning.

The ATV's engine revved as it took off through the forest.

Luke pushed himself up to his feet and got ready to fight.

chapter **TWENTY-FIVE**

Luke looked down at John, who was still doubled over, one hand holding the rifle, the other holding his aching groin. He wished like hell he hadn't left Roy's gun on the ATV's gun rack, but he had, which meant he was unarmed. He would have to go up against an armed man with nothing other than his bare hands. And if he was going to do that, there would be no better time to strike than now, while the asshole wasn't suspecting it.

Rushing forward, Luke grabbed the gun and pulled, hoping John's grip was loose.

It wasn't.

The man, though in a great deal of pain, held firmly to his weapon.

Luke brought up his knee and slammed it against John's nose.

John straightened up and released his groin in exchange for his nose, which was bleeding profusely. "Son of a bitch," he shouted, the words muffled behind his hand.

Luke yanked on the gun again, careful to avoid aiming the thing at himself. It was still no use. John had a death grip on the rifle, even though it was only with one hand.

While Luke was focused on the gun and on avoiding accidentally shooting himself, John let go of his nose long enough to punch Luke in his. Luke didn't see it coming. The pain was immediate and intense, making him forget all about the gun, all about John, about the man-eating animal and Roy and everything else. All he could think about was the blinding pain that radiated out from his nose and spread across his face and throughout his skull. He brought both of his hands up and cupped his nose, feeling the warm, slick blood that oozed from both nostrils. "Son of a damn bitch," he said from behind his hands. "Holy hell, that hurts. Oh my god."

"Yeah, it hurts," John said, using the tips of his fingers to inspect the damage done to his face.

Luke was still reeling from the unsuspected blow. Even in his scrappier days, he'd never experienced a direct punch to the nose that hurt as bad as this one. He kept his eyes squeezed shut to block out the pain, but it did little in the way of helping.

Eventually the aching subsided, and Luke dropped his hands away from his face. He wiped the blood on his pants and spit out all that had gone into his mouth. Then, he looked at John, ready to fight for the gun again.

The gun that was now pointed at his head.

Instinctively, Luke held his hands up, chest high, palms out. "Easy there, John. You don't want to do something you can't take back."

"Shut up! You don't know what I wanna do."

"You're right. I don't. But I can only assume that you're smart enough to know that shooting me would be awfully bad for you."

"Only if I get caught." He grinned. "And I ain't been caught yet."

A chill coursed through Luke's body. Did this guy just admit that he'd killed a person before? Possibly several people?

"What are you really doing out here, John? I get the feeling you're not out here to find that animal."

"No shit, asshole."

"Okay, then. So what *are* you doing out here?"

"I ain't tellin' you shit."

"Alright. But if I don't know what you're doing, I can't exactly help you do it. You know, more hands get the job done faster."

John jerked his head side to side, as if he heard something and was trying to hear it better. But Luke heard nothing. Nothing except the sound of his heart thudding in his chest, sending blood rushing through his ears.

"So," Luke continued, "what do you say? Need some help?"

"I had some help, asshole. Until you came along and ruined it for me." He thrust the gun forward.

Luke flinched, expecting a bullet to come charging out of the barrel. When none did, he said, "What do you mean I ruined it? What did I do?"

"You let him go," John shouted.

"Let who go? I don't know what you're talking about. All I did—"

"All you did was let him go. He was workin' for me. And now he's gone. All because of you!" He stepped forward, thrusting the rifle once again toward Luke.

Luke flinched again, then swallowed around the lump in his throat and tried not to look at the barrel of the gun. "Look, man, I really don't know what you're talking about."

"The kid!"

"The kid? You mean Denny?"

"I don't know his fuckin' name. But he's gone because of you," he spat. His jaw clenched, the muscles visibly working beneath the skin. "My buddy's dead because that fuckin' bear killed him, and now you've let the kid go."

Luke tried to fit all the pieces together and figure out what this guy was talking about. John didn't know the kid's name, but the kid had been helping him. Helping him do what? And how could he not know his name? And what bear?

"Well, that's okay," Luke said calmly. "I'll take his place. I'll help you. I'll do whatever it was he was doing for you. What do you need help with?"

"Oh no," John said, shaking his head. "No way. No fuckin' way! No more adults."

"Why no more adults?"

"I've been screwed over by too many adults to have them help me. Only kids from now on. Kids don't steal. They don't lie and stab you in the back. And they sure as shit don't run off with your woman or your money or your product."

Product? What the hell was he talking about? What prod—*ooooohhh*, Luke thought as the pieces began to click together in his mind.

Product.

Drugs. It had to be drugs. Nobody but drug dealers referred to something as product. And not just people who did drugs, but actual drug dealers. The people moving the stuff, and the ones producing it.

But if John was only moving the drugs, why was he out in the woods? It was possible, albeit unlikely, that he had stashed a bunch of drugs somewhere in the forest, but that seemed like a peculiar place to keep them. Especially during hunting season, when the woods were crawling with people who might find it. Most drug dealers kept their stashes at their house. Probably to avoid it being stolen.

So if he wasn't hiding the drugs, the only other thing he could be doing was making the stuff. And if he was in the woods making drugs, it had to be meth. He must have a meth lab set up somewhere. But Luke hadn't seen any lab. Not that he would know what one looked like if he ever saw one. He'd always assumed it would be unmistakable if he ever did happen upon one. Like one glance at it and he would think *ah yes, this here's a meth lab*. But the only thing he'd seen in the woods tonight was the campsite where he'd found Denny. The one that smelled like the inside of a cat's bladder.

Wait. That was it. It wasn't a hunting campsite at all. It was a meth lab. The camper. The ATV. The table with the pots and pans. The scale. The stench. And Denny. No wonder the kid was so scared.

"Hey, I don't steal," Luke said, calmly trying to keep the conversation going to buy some time until he could figure out what to do next.

"Everybody steals."

"Not me. And I don't do meth, so…"

John's eyes narrowed. "Who said anything about meth?"

"Well, nobody, but I just assumed—"

139

"No you didn't. You're out here lookin' for it, aren't you?"

"No," Luke said, his voice rising with panic. He forced himself to calm down, but if it worked at all, he couldn't tell. "I told you, I'm looking for the animal. Nothing else."

"Yeah, but you said something about meth."

"I misspoke—"

"I didn't say meth. You said meth."

"I know. I know I did. But it was only because you were talking about product and people stealing from you and you needing help...I just assumed it was meth."

"And why would you just assume that?" He leaned his head back and looked down his nose at Luke.

"I don't know. I guess I've watched too much *Breaking Bad*."

John studied Luke for a half a minute, then asked, "What do you know about meth?"

"Damn near nothing. I've never done it. Hell, I've never even seen it. Except on the show."

"That fuckin' show." John shook his head and scoffed. "It's not like that in real life, you know."

"I'm sure it's not. They always make stuff look better on TV."

"You ever cook?"

"I tried to fry some eggs once. They were crunchy on the outside and still liquid on the inside. I usually do the grilling at my house. Hamburgers and hot dogs. Simple stuff. Sometimes they're edible. If you pick off the burned parts."

"No, asshole. Meth. You ever cook meth?"

"Oh. No."

"Well, seein' as how you took my helper away, I think it's time you learned."

"Wait. You want me to cook meth with you?"

"Not with me. This ain't a fuckin' partnership. I'm not Walter White and you ain't Jesse motherfuckin' Pinkman. You're cookin' it for me."

"Are you telling me that you had that little boy cooking your meth?"

"He didn't cook it. He did the other stuff while I cooked it. But I ain't trustin' you to do the other stuff. You'll cook while I weigh it and package it and all that other shit. I told you before. I don't trust adults." He pointed at Luke. "And you are a fuckin' adult."

"Isn't cooking meth..."

"What?"

"I don't know. Dangerous? Doesn't it explode or something?"

"Well yeah. If you fuck it up."

"So..."

"So don't fuck it up. Simple as that."

Sighing, Luke said, "Look, I don't know the first thing about drugs. Especially meth. Frankly, I didn't even want to come out here tonight. I was supposed to be home with my wife and daughter. Then my asshole friend called and asked me to help him find a deer, and that turned into us coming out here to chase a crazed animal...The whole night's been a real fiasco, honestly, and I just want to go home. I'm cold and tired and, hey, I won't say a word about you or your meth. I swear. Not a word to anyone. So what do you say? You go your way, I'll go mine, and this whole thing will be over. Sound good?"

John laughed. "Sound good," he mimicked, and then he roared with laughter. While he was doubled over, Luke looked around for anything that could be used as a weapon. He found nothing. The only limbs on the ground were pencil-thin twigs. The only rocks were nothing more than pebbles.

Like a lone prostitute working a seaside brothel during the Navy's shore leave, he was screwed.

Left with no other options, Luke could only watch as John laughed until he no longer found it funny.

When the guffaws died down, he caught his breath, and then he looked at Luke. "You're so fuckin' stupid, man. But damn if you ain't funny."

"Well you know me," Luke said awkwardly. "I'm a walking chuckle hut."

John laughed again, but not as enthusiastically as he had before.

Luke needed to keep the guy amused until he could find a weapon or a way to subdue him. He didn't think simply running away from the man would do the trick. If this guy used his own product, which all drug dealers did, that meant he was strung out on meth. And though Luke didn't know much at all about the drug, he knew one thing for certain. You could never trust a meth head.

"I think I'm gonna like workin' with you," John said. "That kid was a good worker. Did everything I told him to do. Never said a word. No back talk. Didn't eat much. Didn't bother me. But he was no fun at all. I think me and you are gonna have some fun." He leaned forward and smiled. "Sound good?" he asked, mimicking Luke again. He then laughed as if that was the funniest thing he'd ever heard.

Luke laughed too, though he didn't find it funny at all. He was simply biding his time.

chapter **TWENTY-SIX**

With Tom pointing the way, Denny navigated through the woods, following the beam of the ATV's headlight as he maneuvered around trees and stumps, up and down hills, and through thick underbrush. The boy was by no means a pro at driving the four-wheeler, but he was skilled enough to keep them on all four wheels, and that was something.

Though he had driven away from Luke and John quickly, he'd slowed down a great deal once they were a safe enough distance away, and he had crept along at little more than a snail's pace ever since.

Tom wanted to scream at the kid to hurry the hell up because he was on the verge of dying, but he kept his mouth shut and focused on trying to stay alive and guide the boy back to the truck. Not only because the kid had been through a hell of an ordeal already without some asshole screaming at him to go faster on a machine he wasn't used to driving, but also because he was afraid that if he did start yelling at the boy, the kid would crash the damn thing and kill one or the both of them. And Tom would be super pissed if he survived everything he'd been through in his life only to die in an ATV wreck.

Finally, they made it back to where Tom had parked the truck hours earlier. They came in at the front of the truck, the headlight of the ATV shining on the grill of the old truck and revealing the damage that had been done to it in Tom's absence.

Busted tires.

Bent doors, one of which was laying on the ground.

Dented fenders.

Shards of shattered glass shimmering in the light.

"What the hell...?" Tom muttered as they drove around the truck he'd owned for most of his adult life.

As Denny rolled them along slowly, Tom studied the vehicle and shook his head. It was trashed. Ruined. Beyond repair. Even if he had the money to fix it, which he didn't, he probably wouldn't even bother to take it somewhere and have it restored. He figured it was time to get a new one, though letting the old thing go wasn't going to be easy. It would be akin to losing an old friend.

That truck had been there through every major event in his life. When he'd married, he'd driven his new bride through town with tin cans tied to the back bumper. When she'd given birth to their children, he'd driven them home from the hospital each time in that truck. When their divorce went before the judge, Tom had driven to court in it. He'd then driven from the courthouse to the bar and got drunk off his ass. He'd ran it into a ditch on the way home that night, the scrape on the front passenger fender still there as a testament to the fact. That truck was a part of him. But it was time to let it go, no matter how hard it would be to say goodbye.

Jolted out of his reverie when the ATV stopped rolling, Tom looked over the top of Denny's head, preparing to call out to Roy. But before the words left his mouth, he saw his friend in a grisly battle with the beast, spotlighted by the machine's single headlight.

Tom blinked, then blinked again. He wasn't hallucinating. It was real. Roy was being mauled by the biggest black bear he'd ever seen. It was easily the size of a grizzly bear, though that wasn't possible. But he was looking at it. It was happening. It was killing Roy.

Shit. It was killing Roy.

Roy was on the ground, drenched in blood. He's already dead, Tom thought. There's no way he could be alive. Not after losing that much blood.

The bear stood on its hind legs with Roy's leg dangling from its mouth.

"Holy shit," Tom whispered. He was sure that the bear had ripped Roy's leg off like a drumstick at Thanksgiving. But when the bear shook its head, Tom heard Roy scream. He then saw his friend's body follow the side-to-side movement of the leg and realized that it wasn't detached from the torso. And Roy wasn't dead. At least not yet. But if Tom didn't do something—and fast—both of those things would become true.

Ignoring the blinding pain in his chest, Tom got off the four-wheeler, leaning heavily on Denny for support. He was expecting the pain to intensify when he moved, which it did. What he wasn't expecting was the lightheadedness that overwhelmed him and threatened to take him down. He squinted his eyes, determined to fight both the blackness that loomed at the periphery of his vision and the bear.

He pulled the sling off his shoulder and gripped the rifle in both hands as he stepped closer to where the bear was mauling Roy. Slowly, Tom raised the gun, gritting his teeth against the bolt of pain that shot through his chest, spurred on by the movement.

He tried to put the bear in his crosshairs, but between the actual darkness of the night around him and the inner darkness that wanted to consume him, he couldn't see the crosshairs in the scope. He couldn't even see the sights on the barrel. And with the little bit of strength he had left, he did all he could do, which was pull the trigger and hope for the best.

As soon as the gun fired, Tom cried out and dropped the gun. Half a second later, he fell to the ground beside it and relinquished himself to the pain.

The bullet whizzed past the bear's head, missing the beast by more than a foot. But the sound drew its attention away from Roy and toward Denny, who sat on the four-wheeler, stunned.

The bear let go of Roy and turned. It walked over to Tom and sniffed his body. It pawed at him, and then stood on its back legs, ready to drop on all fours and began ravaging the man's unconscious body.

This time, the bullet hit the bear in the abdomen.

The animal fell back, roaring in anger. It tried to stand, had some difficulty doing so, but managed to get to its feet. It looked at Denny, who sat on the ATV with Roy's rifle—left on the gun rack of the ATV by Luke—clutched tightly in both hands, the barrel aimed at the bear and ready to fire again if necessary. Then, as if sensing it had been defeated, the bear turned and walked away, disappearing into the woods.

Denny watched the bear until he could see it no longer. Then, he turned his head, scanning the woods around him for any sign that it had changed its mind and decided to come back.

Roy coughed, spitting up blood. He'd been teetering between consciousness and unconsciousness, life and death, when the shots had been fired. He wasn't sure who had done the shooting, but he didn't much care. Whatever had happened made the bear stop chewing on him, and he was grateful for that.

He tried to wiggle his toes. Had no idea if it worked.

He tried to move his legs. Wasn't sure whether or not he did.

He rolled his head to the right, toward the area where he thought the shots had been fired. He saw a light. At first, he thought it was *the* light. The one everyone said they saw when they died. But he blinked and realized it wasn't that kind of light. It wasn't shining down from the sky. It was only a few feet off the ground. And it was nowhere near as bright as he figured a heavenly light would be.

It was a headlight.

It took a lot of effort for Roy to raise his head and look down at his body to survey the damage. When he did, he wished like hell he hadn't. He was a mess. All he could see was blood and shredded clothing. No telling what kind of carnage lay beneath all that, and he wasn't sure he wanted to know.

He let his head fall back to the ground and roll to the side once more. He saw a large mass lying on the ground about a dozen paces away from him, near the headlight. He thought it might be the bear, but it wasn't hairy. At least not hairy enough to be a bear.

Roy blinked, coughed up more blood, and blinked again. Then he could see that the mass was Tom.

It took a long time and a lot more effort than Roy thought he could muster, but he eventually managed to pull himself across the cold earth to where his buddy laid.

By god, if they were going to die, at least they would die together.

chapter **TWENTY-SEVEN**

Luke walked slowly through the woods, trying to ignore the gun that was aimed at his back. He couldn't see it, but he could feel it. Just as he could feel John's eyes on him.

"What do you say we go back and get my friends to help us? The more the merrier, I always say," Luke said, though he had never in his life said that. He was just hoping that if John agreed to go back for Tom and Roy, the three could team up and overpower him. But when a burst of laughter came from behind him, Luke knew the man wasn't going to go along with his plan.

"Go back for your friends? You mean the fat guy having the heart attack and the scrawny drunk? I don't think so."

"Well then can we at least go back and get my coat and gloves from Denny? I gave them to him so he wouldn't be cold. Now I'm cold. If I'm going to be out here helping you, then I'll need my coat."

"You'll be fine."

"But I'll freeze to death."

"That's a chance I'm willin' to take."

Of course he was willing to take the chance, Luke thought. He wasn't the one with the chattering teeth.

Luke knew John was taking him back to the so-called camp site, which was really a meth lab, in order to force him to produce the drug. But they were taking a different route than Luke had taken earlier when he'd set out by himself after leaving Tom behind. The terrain along this path was flatter and more level than the way Luke had gone before, but it was much more treacherous, with more rocks and fallen trees and thorny, tangled underbrush. Walking this path didn't wind him as much as the route he'd taken earlier, but it certainly took more effort and concentration for him to not twist an ankle. And though he tripped several times, he managed to stay on his feet.

Unable to maintain the silence, John began to talk. "You don't know how hard it is to find a kid these days. Everyone's so worried about their kids being snatched, they keep a pretty close eye on them. Like hawks, actually. And it isn't like it used to be, where kids walked everywhere they went. No, they gotta have Mommy and Daddy drive them everywhere they go. Makes it damn near impossible for a guy like me to grab one without a big deal being made about it. But I finally find one, after weeks of searching, and then you come along and take him away from me in the blink of an eye."

"Are you saying you kidnapped Denny?"

"What do you think, smart guy? You think I just found him out here in the woods waitin' on me? Of course I kidnapped him. Although, that's a bit of a strong word, really. I'm just...borrowin' him for a while. I'll take him back when I'm done with him."

"When will that be?"

John thought before saying, "I don't know. I'm makin' good money, so I have no plans of stoppin' anytime soon. But I reckon eventually I'll let him go. He'll be too big to keep around. Once he gets so big, he'll get to thinkin' he can run off. I can't have that. I can't have him tellin' what he knows. I ain't goin' to prison."

A horrible question crept into Luke's mind, one that he didn't want to know the answer to but felt that he needed to ask anyway. "You didn't, you know, mess with the boy, did you?"

"What? Jesus. No. God no. What kind of sick fuck do you take me for?"

"Well, I didn't take you for a kidnapper when I first met you, and I was wrong about that, so…"

"Trust me. I ain't never messed with no kid. I don't do that. He works for me, and nothin' else." John paused, then asked, "Do you mess with kids?"

"Hell no," Luke nearly shouted. "And I'd kill any son of a bitch who did."

"Alright. Settle down. Damn. Don't get your tits in a tither. I was just askin' because you asked me. I thought maybe you wanted to swap stories or somethin'."

Luke had plenty more he wanted to say on the subject, but he reminded himself that the guy had a gun pointed at his back. If he was going to get shot, Luke would much rather it be because he had tried to wrestle the gun away from him than because he mouthed off.

Instead of saying something that might send a bullet through his spine, Luke said, "Well, I don't."

The two walked in silence for a couple of minutes before John asked, "Did you guys ever find that bear?"

Luke almost asked John what bear he was talking about, but then the pieces suddenly slammed together, and it all made sense. The monster wasn't a monster at all. It was a bear. John had known this all along, probably because it had killed his buddy back at their camp site that wasn't a camp site.

Luke said, "No. Not after the time we told you about when we first met you."

"Hm," was all John said in response.

There were still pieces of the puzzle missing, so Luke said, "Hey, when you said that animal had been nothing but trouble, what did you mean?"

"What do you think I meant?"

"You could've meant that it had been a lot of trouble to people in the county. People whose property has been damaged or whose pets have been killed. Certainly, a lot of trouble for your brother. But I got the feeling that's not what you were talking about." Luke stumbled, nearly fell. After regaining his footing, he continued, "You made it…I don't know…it sort of sounded like you knew the bear. Like it has caused you, personally, a lot of problems."

"It has. I thought if I got it young enough and trained it right, it'd be fine. And I did get it young enough. Stole it right out of the den when it was a baby. There were two of them there, sleepin' next to their momma, and I thought about takin' both of them. But I wasn't sure I could handle two bears. So I took one and figured if it worked out alright, I'd get another one the next year. But this one's been such a damn handful, I haven't even bothered going back for another one."

"So you've raised this bear from a cub?"

"Yup."

"But it's huge. It's much bigger than a normal black bear."

"Yeah." John chuckled. "That's just about the only thing that worked out right."

"You mean you made it big? How?"

"Steroids."

That explained a lot.

"And meth."

"What?" Luke spun around and faced John, who was taken by surprise. His eyes widened, and he jumped back a step. "You gave that bear meth?"

"Yeah."

"Are you fucking insane?"

"What's the big deal?"

"What's the big deal?" Luke pressed his hands against his forehead, his mouth open. "You don't see what the big deal is? You gave a *bear* steroids *and* meth. Now, not only is there a big ass bear running around killing people, but it's all hopped up on drugs. Are you crazy? What the hell is wrong with you?" Even as Luke asked the question, he knew the answer. The man was using drugs himself. His brain was addled with the effects of meth. Most likely, it was just a pile of goo sloshing around inside the man's skull. Not thinking. Not processing the ramifications of his actions. Never thinking. Just doing.

"Dude, chill out. I'll find it. And when I do…"

"What? What will happen when you find it?"

"I don't know. I'll stop giving it meth, I guess."

"Oh my god," Luke said, throwing his hands up before letting them fall to his sides. "Unbelievable. This is just…just unbelievable."

"What? Isn't that what you want?"

"The only thing worse than you giving it drugs is for you to *stop* giving it drugs. You can't just stop cold turkey like that. Who knows what the damn thing will do? Withdrawals, I imagine. And I'm sure that'll go well. Jesus."

"Well what do you want me to do?"

"I want you to not feed a wild animal steroids and meth," Luke shouted. "Damn it to hell, John. What were you thinking?"

John raised the gun, aimed it at Luke's face. Staring down the barrel of a loaded gun in the hands of an unstable dope head brought Luke to his senses. He suddenly didn't worry so much about the bear. He was focused more on keeping the bullets out of his body.

Luke took a deep breath to calm himself, and said, "Okay. Look, we can figure this out together. I'll help you find the bear. I'll help you make the meth. Whatever you need me to do. Just, just calm down."

"Oh, I'm calm," John said with a smile. "I ain't worried about the bear. It'll find its way back to camp. It always does. But that meth won't make itself. So let's go." He thrust the gun toward Luke to indicate he should start walking.

Luke turned, expecting to hear the rifle fire at any second. When the sound didn't come, he kept walking.

Minutes later, Luke said, "I need to take a leak."

John ignored him. Or maybe he hadn't heard what he said.

Luke repeated himself.

This time, John said, "I heard you the first time."

"I'm going to stop and take a piss," Luke said, tired of waiting for John's permission to urinate. Luke looked left, then right. He found a tree big enough to conceal him and headed toward it.

"Whoa, there, fella. Where you think you're going?"

"I told you. I need to piss."

"So do it right there. Right where you are."

"I can't go if you're going to watch me."

"Then you must not need to go that bad."

Sighing, Luke asked, "Could you at least turn around while I go?"

John lowered the gun. "Fine. But if you try to run, I'll shoot you. And if you do manage to get away from me, I'll go straight back to where your fat friend is, and I'll shoot him. And the boy.

And your scrawny friend too. You just think about that before you go trying anything stupid." He then turned his back to Luke.

Luke kept his eyes on John. As soon as the man turned around, Luke bent down and picked up the rock that had caught his eye. It was perfect for what he intended to do with it. It was big, but not so big that Luke couldn't hold it in his hands. It was heavy, but not so heavy that he couldn't swing it.

Gripping the rock tightly in both hands, he quietly snuck up behind John. He raised the rock high above his head, and then brought it down fast, slamming it against the man's skull.

There was a cracking sound, and John fell to the ground, dropping the gun in the process.

Luke let the rock fall from his hands as he stepped around John's body. He didn't believe he'd killed him. He hadn't even intended to kill him. But he figured—and hoped—the guy was unconscious, at the very least.

Bending down, Luke reached for the rifle. His fingers touched the wooden stock. But then John's hand suddenly wrapped around his wrist, squeezing tightly with his long, bony ice-cold fingers.

Luke then reached for the gun with his left hand, but John grabbed that one too. Jerking, Luke pulled free of the man's grasp and started to run, foregoing the weapon. If he could make it back to the truck before John caught up to him, he could use either Roy's or Tom's rifle to keep him subdued until the police could arrest him.

He took a step.

John grabbed at his ankle, tripping him.

Luke fell, bracing himself with his hands just before colliding with the ground.

Rolling onto his back, Luke kicked at John until he broke free of his hold, then he stood up to run. Just as he pushed himself up from the ground, he felt the other man's weight come crashing down onto his back, his arms winding around Luke's neck. They fell to the ground with Luke's face in the dirt and John atop him.

John squeezed his arms tight against Luke's neck, cutting off his air supply.

Luke rolled side to side, trying to shake the man off his back. When that failed, he hooked his fingers between his throat and

John's arms, trying to gain enough leverage to pull his arms away. It was no use. The man had one hell of a grip on him.

It can't end like this, Luke thought.

It won't end like this.

If Susan was going to have to spend the rest of her life telling the story of how she became a widow, that story damn sure wouldn't be about how her husband was choked to death by a drugged-up meth head.

Using his fist, Luke punched beside his head, hoping to connect with John's eye or nose or jaw, anything that would bring him pain and make him let go. The first couple of blows hit nothing but air. The third one hit something.

"Ow. What the hell did you do that for?" John asked, as if Luke had hit him out of the blue and for no good reason.

Instead of answering, which he couldn't have done anyway for lack of air, Luke punched again, his fist glancing the side of John's head.

"Stop it," John hissed.

Luke punched again, felt his knuckles collide with John's nose. It wasn't a great hit. With the punch being thrown at such an odd angle, there was hardly any force behind it, but since John's beak had already taken a hit earlier, it didn't take much to elicit a howl of pain and a fresh stream of blood pouring from his nostrils.

That was the hit that did the trick. Just as Luke was beginning to see white flecks dancing in the periphery of his vision, John let go and rolled off Luke's back.

Luke clutched his neck, coughing and gasping for air while John cupped his hands around his nose and cussed.

As soon as Luke caught his breath, he pushed himself up to his feet and took off running. Behind him, John shouted for him to stop. He called him names, most of which would've made any sailor blush. But Luke kept running, not looking back.

At least not until the shot rang out.

chapter **TWENTY-EIGHT**

Luke felt it before he heard it. The searing pain tearing through his shoulder like a hot bolt of lightning. He stopped running, shocked at what had happened. He'd been shot. The son of a bitch had actually shot him.

With his left hand, he reached across his chest and touched his right shoulder. It was warm and wet. Sticky with blood. It smelled like copper, and it hurt like hell. He couldn't tell how bad it was, but with that much blood covering his arm in such a short amount of time, he knew it couldn't be good.

Wincing, sucking in a lungful of air through gritted teeth, Luke applied pressure to the wound, using his hand to slow the bleeding. It hurt, but not as much as dying probably would. He had to get the hell out of there before the crazy bastard shot him again and he was forced to find out which was the greater pain.

Veering to the right, Luke ran again. He wasn't fast now, unable to use his arms to keep his balance and to keep the tree limbs from slapping against his face. But any progress was good progress, so he kept going, zigging and zagging through the woods, keeping as low as he could and trying to make himself a harder target to hit.

Another shot came, taking a chunk of bark off a large oak tree as Luke ran past it. He ducked instinctively but didn't look back. He wanted to, but he kept his eyes focused on the ground in front of him and continued moving forward.

Thinking of Susan.

Of Hope.

Of all they still had to do together.

And how he was never, ever going to step foot in the woods again if he made it through this. Not for camping. Not for hunting. Not for finding morel mushrooms. Not for anything.

Another shot came from closer behind him. Much closer. The bullet kicked up dirt beside Luke. If this John guy was a better shot, Luke would be dead by now.

Thankfully he was no Annie Oakley.

Luke tripped but didn't fall.

He ran blindly into limbs that slapped against his cheeks, leaving scratches in their wake.

And he did it all while clutching his shoulder, trying to force the blood to stay inside his body.

"Make it easy on yourself," John shouted from behind Luke. "If you stop runnin' now, I won't kill you. But if you keep runnin', I'm gonna kill you *and* your friends."

Luke didn't stop. He did risk looking back, though. He glanced behind him, over his injured shoulder. He saw John bring the rifle up to his face and send another shot headed his way.

Trying to dodge the bullet, Luke jumped to the left, hoping to put a tree between him and the piece of metal that was coming for him. But what he found behind the tree was a different kind of metal. The kind that almost made him wish for the bullet instead.

As soon as his left foot came down and the metal teeth of the bear trap snapped shut, clamping onto his calf, Luke fell. He cried out in agony, howling in pain and writhing on the ground. Dead leaves crunched beneath him as he rolled from side to side, trying to shut out the horrific feeling of the rusty metal spikes that penetrated his clothing and skin and dug deep into his flesh.

The pain was something Luke had never experienced before. Like heavy hammers and sharp knives slamming repeatedly and constantly against his lower leg. In comparison, the bullet wound in his shoulder was nothing more than a mosquito bite.

The anguish consumed Luke so completely, he no longer paid attention to John.

Not until he was standing over Luke with the rifle aimed at his face.

John laughed. "I see you found one of my traps. Hurts like a bitch, don't it?"

Luke reached down and gingerly felt his leg, using only his fingertips. Everywhere a piece of metal poked him was wet with blood. None of them were bleeding like his shoulder, but they were bleeding all the same. He figured that once the metal spikes were pulled out of his flesh—*if* they were pulled out—the bleeding would intensify because there would be nothing to plug the holes. The many, many holes that were now in his leg.

"I told you not to run. But you did. So now, I'm going to kill you, and then I'm going to go find your friends and kill them too. And as for the kid. Well, I reckon I'll just take him back to camp with me. Maybe I'll tie him up this time. Make sure he don't run off again. I sure hate it when folks run off." John pressed his face to the butt of the gun and prepared to pull the trigger. "Any last words?" he asked.

Through gritted teeth, Luke said, "Yeah. Fuck you, asshole."

John laughed. "That's cute. But save it for the devil." He applied pressure with his finger, pulling back on the trigger slowly and allowing just enough time for Luke to see his life flash before his eyes.

Hanging out with his friends.

Meeting Susan for the first time.

Their first date.

Their first kiss.

Their wedding.

The baby.

Hope's first day of school.

Vacations.

Trips.

Lovemaking.

All of it entered his mind and left almost immediately, passing through quickly but lingering just long enough to bring about a sense of peace and calm to Luke and ease the pain that radiated throughout his body. He felt as if Susan and Hope were there with him, hugging him, kissing him, and telling him that everything would be okay because they loved him so much.

He thought about looking away or closing his eyes, but he decided that if this asshole was going to kill him, he would have to look Luke in the eyes and do it.

And then, just as the gun fired, the bear, which neither man had seen approaching, slammed into John, knocking him to the ground and sending the bullet flying high into the air.

Luke's life was spared. For now, at least.

From the ground, he watched in shock as the bear attacked John. He saw the man try to fight back, and then he looked away, no longer able to stomach bearing witness to such a gruesome scene. No matter how much the asshole deserved it.

This was Luke's chance—most likely the last one he would have—to get away. As soon as the bear finished with John, it would turn to him. But he didn't plan to be there when it did.

Luke sat up and began to work on prying the jaws of the bear trap apart. It wasn't easy. The spring was tight, and he didn't have much strength in his right arm now, but he eventually managed to free himself from the thing.

He stood, found the gun that John had dropped when the bear rushed him, and he picked it up. He checked to see how many rounds were left. Enough to do the job, he figured.

Luke raised the rifle, but then he hesitated.

John had done this to himself. He stole the bear from its mother, raised it on a steady diet of steroids, meth, and—most likely—abuse. Everything this animal did to him was of his own doing. Luke wanted to let the bear finish. He wanted it to get the justice that it desired. To destroy the man who had ruined its life.

He thought of leaving, of just turning his back and walking away, leaving the bear to deal with John in peace. But he couldn't do that because he knew that once the bear was done with John Ramshaw, it wouldn't stop there. Its bloodlust wouldn't be quenched just by killing the man who had turned it into such a monster. It would go on to kill again and again. Innocent people would die, children among them.

Luke knew what he had to do.

Aiming at the bear's back, Luke fired a shot and watched it enter the beast's fur.

It roared and turned to face him.

Luke aimed at its head and pulled the trigger. The impact sent bits of hair and flesh and bone flying through the air.

Another roar. This time, it ended with a whimper.

Luke fired again.

And again.

He fired until the bear dropped to the ground and fell on its side, unmoving.

Then, he fired again.

He fired until he was certain that the thing was dead.

Luke looked from the bear to John's mangled body and knew instantly that the man was dead.

Luke dropped the gun and ran once again through the forest, applying pressure to his shoulder and limping on his injured leg. But he ran as fast as his body would carry him, making his way away from the dead man and the monster he created and toward help.

It took what felt like an eternity for Luke to make his way back to the truck, back to where this whole damn nightmare had begun so many hours before.

He saw the headlight of the ATV cutting a beam through the trees, and he followed it, limping on a leg that hurt more and more with each step he took.

Denny was sitting on the four-wheeler, tightly holding a gun and keeping watch on the woods around them.

Luke stopped and leaned against a tree. "You watching for the bear?"

The boy nodded.

"You don't have to. It's dead."

Denny didn't move. He stared at Luke as if he wasn't sure whether or not to believe the thing wouldn't be coming back.

"I promise. It's dead. I killed it."

Believing him now, the boy placed the gun in the rack and put his hands in the pocket of Luke's coat.

Looking around, Luke saw the damaged truck and blood everywhere. A panic rose in him then as he realized that Roy was probably dead. And for that matter, Tom probably was too. But then he heard Roy cough and spit.

Pushing himself away from the tree, Luke limped around until he found Roy and Tom, lying next to each other on the ground. He walked over and stood at their heads, looking down at them.

The two laid side by side, shoulder to shoulder, both staring up into the night sky.

Roy looked bad. If he hadn't coughed, Luke would've been certain that he was dead. His flesh was mangled, his limbs destroyed, and he was covered in blood. Clearly, the bear had got to him.

Tom was beyond pale, but at least he hadn't been mauled by the bear.

"What's this?" Luke asked. "I'm out there fighting with that bear, and you two clowns are back here stargazing like a couple of young lovers."

Tom looked up at Luke and smiled weakly. "I've been wonderin' where you went to, glory hog."

"Hey, you wanted to find the bear," Luke said. "I found the damn thing."

"Did it get you?" Tom asked.

"No. But that son of a bitch John did. Shot me once in the arm. Then I stepped in a damn bear trap of his. But the bear got him for me. Then I got the bear."

"Good for you," Tom said.

"Good," was all Roy could manage to say.

Luke dropped to his knees, and then laid down alongside the two men. He looked up at the sky. It was getting lighter. It seemed he was going to live to see the dawn after all.

In the distance, he heard sirens making their way closer.

"It's about damn time," Tom said.

"Yeah," Luke agreed. "It's a good thing it wasn't an emergency."

The men laughed, and though it wasn't as easy as it used to be, it felt better than it ever had.

AFTERWORD

I recently held a benefit for my mother in-law, Anita. She's battling lung cancer for the second time. It's her third time fighting cancer, and each time has drained her physically and financially.

Hence, the benefit.

One of the things I did for the benefit was sell the opportunity to be a main character in a book. I planned to auction it during the live auction portion of the benefit, but then I remembered that I had a huge fan in Luke Davis. I went to his wife Susan, and we struck a deal behind his back. She donated money to the cause, and I wrote a book for Luke. Huge surprise to him, I'm sure. (Hi, Luke. Hope you enjoy the story.)

I tell you that to tell you this.

Anita is still fighting. We almost lost her shortly after the benefit, but she's not one to go quietly into that good night. However, the war is taking its toll. If you would like to donate money to her for the expenses she's incurring (doctor bills, trips to chemo, etc.), please send them to me via Paypal (kimberlyabettes@yahoo.com) or Facebook, and I will see that she gets them. For other forms of payment, you can email me or contact me through any of my social media accounts. Every little bit helps, as I'm sure you know. Thank you so much.

Kim

ABOUT THE AUTHOR

Kimberly A. Bettes is the author of several novels and short stories. She lives with her husband and son in the beautiful Ozark Mountains of southeast Missouri, where she terrorizes residents of a small town with her twisted tales. It's there she likes to study serial killers and knit. Serial killers who knit are her favorites.

-NOVELS-
The Faceless
Exodus
The Criers Club
The Day Bob Greeley Died
Before the Harvest
RAGE
The Good Neighbor
Annie's Revenge

-HELD SERIES-
Held
Pushed
22918

-NOVELLAS-
In Her Skin
Night Falls
The Cabin on Calhoun Ridge
Shiners

-SHORT STORIES-
Dead Man's Chair
Transference
The Kindness of Strangers
The Hunger
His Ashes
The Home

-COLLECTIONS-
The Shorts
Once Upon a Rhyme
Twisted

-MINUTES TO DEATH SERIES-
The Loneliest Road
Close to Home
The Last Resort
Shock Rock
The French Quarter

-ANTHOLOGIES-
Carnage: After the End Volume 1
Legends of Urban Horror: A Friend of a Friend Told Me

-ESSAYS-
Everybody Wants to Write a Book

Made in the USA
Middletown, DE
14 March 2020